TORA BARRY

FUNERAL OF THE SARDINE

An Atticus Drake Mystery : Book 2

Tora Barry

Published in 2015 by Castleforge Books Ltd

ISBN: 978-09932939-4-8

Chapter One

As the doors of the plane opened, Atticus, halfway back in row sixty-something of Economy Class, remembered. He remembered the thrill of clean hot air swirling through a cabin of overheated stale humankind, bringing with it the smell of a foreign country with a very different climate. He remembered what it was like to be Away, Somewhere Else, and he remembered how fabulous it was.

He put his copy of Sir Francis Chichester's autobiography, *The Lonely Sea and the Sky* in the pocket of his linen blazer and waited patiently for everyone else to climb over the seats and shove one another aside. He had picked up *The Lonely Sea* a couple of days ago, in the lovely Stanfords travel bookshop in Covent Garden, thinking he might learn a few tips, but had barely had a chance to look at it on the flight, thanks to the non-stop activity of his fellow travellers.

Despite the inevitable scramble to get off the plane, Atticus allowed himself to experience a moment of pure bliss. It was good to be out of England, with its grey February sky and its air of austerity. Whatever it was Salty Clark wanted, he'd picked a top time to request a reunion.

A change is as good as a rest, as Ma was always saying. But Atticus's life had been a bit short of change recently.

The last couple of years had been pretty stressful. What had come to be known in the family as The Flora Thing, still preyed on his mind, but had almost been eclipsed by the events of last autumn, when what he had thought would be a delightful affair with a beautiful girl in Venice, had turned into something of a nightmare. But he had come through it, and with the help of Hilly, Hal and the twins, and a Christmas full of domesticity, good cooking and a case or so of excellent Bordeaux, he had been optimistic that the New Year would bring with it a host of new opportunities.

However, the only opportunity which had presented itself up to this point, was a bit of private tutoring which his brother-in-law had found for him. Hal was a counsellor, talking to troubled and under-achieving children, and he usually had a few extremely grateful parents and school heads who were happy to accept a recommendation, when looking for a bit of one-to-one catch-up teaching for their charges. Atticus, with his acceptable History degree from Cambridge, and his distinct lack of any serious career, was perfect for the job.

This time however, he had to admit he had got a bit bogged down with it. The pupils were a small group of sullen teenagers whose parents had clubbed together in a last-ditch attempt to see some return for years of expensive education which had been risked on an illicit drug-fuelled weekend in Brighton. The school had threatened expulsion, Hal had recommended keeping them busy, and Atticus had been drafted in to push them through their GCSEs.

On top of that, it had rained for eight weeks non-stop, and as the school was in Islington, and he still lived in Docklands, he had scarcely seen his own apartment in the daylight since his return from Venice. There was no doubt about it, Salty's call had been most welcome.

Chapter Two

"Bloody *hell* it's hot."

Barry, recently disembarked from row seventy three, barged his way back against the tide through the Arrivals Hall with a luggage trolley, towards his hot sticky family, just as Roger, his scrawny seven-year-old, dragged the first of their gigantic suitcases off the conveyor belt, narrowly avoiding being crushed to death underneath it.

"What did you expect, it's the bloody Canaries! You'd be complaining if it was pigging freezing and pissing down, wouldn't you?" snapped Shell, Barry's wife, who was somehow managing to look sunburnt already, despite not having left the airport. Her face was red, and blotches spread across her neck and shoulders. Barry told himself that she was tired. She needed this holiday. They both did. Although the cost of it was bothering him. He just hadn't managed to find the right time to tell her about the redundancy.

"Well *help him*, can't you?" shouted Shell, as Roger abandoned the first case and clambered onto the conveyor belt, followed by five year-old Tyne. In the distance, Bex, their ten-year old was leaning against a plate glass window, looking out at the tarmac which stretched across the landscape to the sea, and texting someone she referred to as her 'Bezzie'.

"What the hell's *in* all these?" said Barry, piling case onto case. "Did we leave *anything* at home?"

"You wouldn't know if we did or we didn't," said Shell, dragging her sons back from the brink of being sent down the luggage chute back towards the plane and shoving a bag of crisps each into their clammy hands. "Left it all to me as usual. If it was up to you, we'd be here without any stuff at all."

Barry pushed the trolley toward the passport control line ahead of his family, who left a trail of crushed crisps as they went. He thought they'd manage fine without any stuff at all. After all,what did you need for a week in the sun? T-shirt, swimming cozzie, sandals, beer money, that'd do it. He caught Bex's eye as he turned round to check they were all there, and gave her a wink. She rolled her eyes. She was doing that a lot lately, and he didn't know what it was about. It didn't feel that great though.

"Awww, look at them!" said Liv, from row ninety four, hanging onto her boyfriend and hindering his attempts to walk in a straight line through the terminal. "That'll be us one day, won't it? You, me and a pile of cute kids?"

Rob took her face in his hands and planted a lingering kiss on her neat little lips. Behind them the rest of the crowd was forced to stop, backing up like traffic on a motorway. As he pushed his tongue round her tiny fruit-flavoured mouth, he shut his eyes and tried to blot out the vision of Barry and Shell, worn out by life and childcare, and barely able to speak to one another without a snap or a sigh. 'That'll be us' Liv had said. God, he hoped not. He pushed her shoulder strap down and reached a hand almost to her breast before the crowd surged onward. "You," said Liv fondly, snaking her hand round his back and into the gap between the waistband of his underpants and his belt.

"Disgusting," said a smart woman in a breton shirt and huge designer sunglasses, while her two matching teenage daughters sniggered and pointed.

Atticus reached the baggage reclaim and stood a little way away, watching the seething mass as he waited for his holdall to appear. It was an ever-present dilemma whether to check in baggage which might reappear in pieces, or worse, not at all, or carry it onto the plane, which wore you out before you even got to your destination. But nothing could upset Atticus this afternoon, as he savoured the sound of foreign words over the airport's tannoy system, and smelt the myriad scents of a foreign land. Coffee, dry dust, strange food, and beyond, in the hot distance, the smell of the sea.

He retrieved his bag, noting the new scratches and the still-intact padlock, and praised Hilly's great taste in luggage. Its first outing had been the all-expenses trip to Venice from which it, and he, had been lucky to return. This was an altogether different experience for both of them. "One old chair and half a candle, one old jug without a handle," he said to himself, as he found the shoulderstrap in the outside pocket and reattached it. Not for him the five-suitcase tower of Barry and Shell, or the matching pink wheelie-cases of Rob and Liv. He was just a free traveller, in a big, sunshiny world.

At the end of the snaking line of British people going on holiday, Atticus raised his panama hat to the sweaty officials, answered the usual questions about knives and farm animals, and then, quite suddenly, he was swept up in the tide of people, and carried out into the car park.

Chapter Three

The first impression of any of the Canary Islands via their airports is that of a Middle Eastern war zone. There is invariably a car park filled with battered dusty vehicles, and beyond that, rows of struggling palms, battered by hot winds. Beyond *that*, are a few rows of half-finished buildings, concrete blocks, some optimistic lines of washing and further still, dry red rock, banking up and up towards the solid blue sky.

Atticus smiled the smile of a happy man. This was just the beginning and he was going to enjoy himself. He turned away from the open mouths of twenty or thirty coaches, and headed for the taxi rank, where half a dozen elderly Mercedes waited, engines running, for their drivers to emerge from the bar. A queue of single travellers like himself, those who were not on a package holiday, or in an excitable group, built up slowly.

Two lightly tanned women in matching navy skirts, white shirts and yellow scarves stood, side-by-side beaming at the soggy white people spilling towards the coaches. Beside them was a gangly, pale-faced man in the masculine equivalent of their uniform, which was different only in as much as the skirt was trousers and the scarf was a cravat.

Jules pulled at the cravat to relieve his itching neck, "Friday again," he said, "Another week in Sodding Paradise."

"Cheer up," said Amy, "You've only been here a couple of months. I've been here four years. Remember you could be working behind the counter at Lloyds somewhere like Huddersfield." She pulled at her nylon skirt which was riding up over her somewhat generous figure and threatened to cut off the circulation round her thighs.

"Then you'd look like that," added Sooze, pointing out a particularly pale pair of women dragging their cases through the doors. "I hope they're here for a fortnight. It'll take at least that long to get those two warmed up."

"Bet they're mine," said Jules, gloomily, "I always get the grey ones."

"Whereas *I*," said Amy, her attention diverted to the next group coming from the Baggage Reclaim Hall, "Am positive that these are *all mine!*"

The others followed her gaze to where eight extremely good-looking men in surf shorts and tight T-shirts were re-grouping after their flight. There was a great deal of 'high-fiving' and general clowning going on, but that didn't deter Amy, who had undone another button of her shirt to reveal a most welcoming bosom, and was heading towards them, her best smile painted firmly on, and her hand outstretched. "Like bloody Princess Diana," grumbled Sooze behind her. Sooze, at almost five feet ten and lacking any real curves at all, did up *her* top button and fashioned the scarf into more of a Margaret Thatcher bow. "Authority," she said, "that's what we *should* be demonstrating here."

"On behalf of Cupcake Tours, may I say, Welcome to Tenerife?" said Amy, her blue eyes trained directly on the most handsome of them all. "Are you with me?"

Jules and Sooze carried on with their administrative duties, ticking holidaymakers off their lists as they came through the gates and assigning them to the coaches which would take them to their hotels and villas along the coast, commiserating with the moaners, joking with the jollier ones, and managing the drunks, who had begun with beer at eight in the morning in Manchester and were still hard at it, at three.

"You haven't experienced a Fiesta yet have you?" Sooze asked, as she and Jules hauled overstuffed suitcases into the luggage hold of one of the coaches while the driver leant against the side of his vehicle and watched.

"No," admitted Jules, "I haven't been here long enough. I *think* I'm looking forward to it. But to be honest it does sound a bit weird." He dragged the last of the suitcases off a trolley and into the coach. "This is like feeding a whale," he added, "What the *hell* do they put in these?"

"*Entierro de la Sardina*," Sooze said, "Funeral of the Sardine. It's one of the islands' more eccentric customs. They build a huge fish out of papier mache, and everyone dresses up as if they're going to a funeral. The men in particular go for the widows' outfits, all black dresses and veils, and a fair bit of stocking and suspender action, and then everyone parades the fish through the streets and down to the sea, where they set fire to it. Why is it, that when women dress up as men, they just go for suits and ties, but when men dress as women they have to go the whole hog with the underwear?"

Jules shrugged. "Don't know. It's a boy thing. Or at least a certain type of boy." He slammed the hatch of the coach shut and prayed it wouldn't burst open on the motorway, strewing customers' luggage across three carriageways.

"Well you'll certainly enjoy the widows then," said Sooze, "But I should warn you, things can get a bit hairy."

"And I'm guessing you don't just mean the stocking-wearing, bearded widows," said Jules.

The Arrivals Hall was almost clear again, and cleaning staff were sweeping up and replacing trolleys in readiness for the next inbound flight from Stansted in just under an hour. The taxi drivers had already begun to return from their first round trips and the bar was filling up. "Come on," said Jules, "Let's get a drink before the next rush. I could murder a *cafe cortado*."

"And talking of murder," said Sooze suddenly, "Look...."

Jules followed her gaze into the car park. A sleek black limousine drew to a halt by a side entrance. Several man in dark suits and sunglasses came out of the airport and got into the car before it swept away, its blacked-out windows allowing Jules and Sooze no glimpse of who was inside it.

"Who do you think that is?" said Jules.

Sooze looked at him. "There are some things we just don't ask," she said. "You'll pick that up quite quickly too."

Behind them, Atticus's driver finally reclaimed his cab and drove him away in a cloud of dust and cheap aftershave, to the tinny beat of Spanish radio.

"El Puerto, por favor," Atticus said to the driver's vast damp back. Over his shoulder, Atticus could see the tattered photographs of several gap-toothed children, framed by strings of rosary beads and sprigs of what might once have been rosemary. "El Puerto?" Atticus said again, hopefully.

Chapter Four

The rattling Mercedes shot along the island's one motorway at speed, veering from lane to lane in the wake of delivery lorries and tankers making their way up from the docks a few miles behind them, interspersed with tractors ambling along at five miles an hour. The driver had the radio on at full volume and all the windows open to save the cost of running the car's air conditioning. Atticus's attention was taken up with ducking small bits of road debris thrown in at him, while he gripped the armrest which was so well-worn the cracked black leather was spilling out orange foam in alien form. "Adventure," he said to himself over and over. "If I die, I will do so in the throes of an adventure."

From time to time the driver yelled something over his shoulder. Atticus could only nod and watch his own hot, scared reflection in the rear view mirror.

After about twenty minutes, the driver suddenly flung the wheel to the left and the car shot up a slip road, clipping a roundabout at the top and veering off over the brow of a hill. Atticus briefly glimpsed a row of shops, maybe a supermarket, and pedestrians throwing themselves sideways as the car roared past, round a long circular bend and down, down, down. The taxi screeched to a stop and Atticus hit the floor. There was a long silence.

He picked himself up from the mess of cigar ash and sweet wrappers in the footwell. Opening the door of the car he was surprised to find that they hadn't crashed at all, but instead the car had come to a stop, just, and only just, short of a small and frankly inadequate row of bollards marking the edge of the harbour. The bright blue water at low tide, was just four feet below. Across the marina he could see the stone breakwaters which marked the harbour entrance, and beyond, he saw the sea meet the equally brilliantly blue sky. Across the harbour itself, everything was white. Rows and rows of sleek white yachts and motorboats, bobbing up and down in the warm but lively wind, pulling at their mornings, their rigging making clinking and clanking music that Atticus knew he would never hear again without being reminded of this moment.

Hauling his own bag out of the boot of the car and retrieving his jacket from the crumpled heap of oily rags which accompanied it, he handed some Euros over to the driver who pocketed them and drove off, scattering a small selection of bicycles.

On leaving home, Atticus had chosen his wardrobe carefully, aiming for 'seasoned traveller who may find himself aboard a yacht'. Now he was in the presence of the potential yacht, he felt very overdressed. Around him young men in beach shorts and deck shoes hopped about on boats, whilst women in tiny cotton dresses and bare feet wandered up and down hoping to attract attention. His back had begun to ache with the pressure of the long flight and a series of near road accidents, and he was badly in need of a drink. In his pocket, Sir Francis Chichester had suffered a crushing blow too and its cover needed a good smoothing down, preferably alongside a gin and tonic.

Trying not to look too much like an Edwardian tourist, he consulted his phone for Salty's instructions.

Pantalon 8 Far end. *The Cangreco Loco.* **If I'm not there, climb aboard and settle in. We'll catch up later. Salty.**

Pantalon? *Trousers?* No, that was French. This was Spanish. Atticus pretended he was making a call while accessing the phone's translator. *Pantalon.* Pontoon. Pier. *Aha.*

He followed the edge of the harbour until he reached Pier number 8. As he stepped down onto it the wooden slats shifted and rocked under his feet. This sailing lark was going to take some getting used to.

The *Cangreco Loco* was moored at the end of the pier, and Atticus had to negotiate the full length of the moving platform, stepping carefully over the mass of mooring lines, discarded fenders and hosepipes to get there. He stood for a while, facing the shifting wall of shiny white fibreglass which was the side of Salty's boat and wondering how the hell he was supposed to get on it.

He put out a hand and grabbed a section of deck rail. The boat lurched towards him, and he let go. Then he put down his bag, and using both hands, tried his weight. The lurch was more pronounced this time, and he managed to get one foot up onto the deck. As the boat righted itself, it took Atticus with it, so that he was hanging half upside down from the side. He let go, landing on his bag on the pontoon with a crash which reverberated right back up to the gate.

He thought he heard laughing from somewhere, and standing up, tried to look as though he had been watching someone else make a complete and utter fool of themselves.

Perhaps he would just go back to the road, find a cafe and wait for Salty. But then again that would just stave off the moment when he had to get onto the bloody boat, and next time, he wouldn't be alone. He decided to try again. It had to be possible. People did it all the time. Everywhere there were people on boats, cleaning them, hosing down decks, sitting with drinks, tinkering with gadgets, mucking about with ropes. They must all get on and off all the time.

He took a firmer hold of the deck rail, pulled it towards him with both hands, and waited until the boat calmed down. Then using the spring of the pontoon as a launchpad, he hauled himself upwards. At which point he was hanging over the side of the boat again, although mercifully this time he was the right way up. As his arms began to burn with the strain of holding his weight, he realised he was no better off. Letting go, he fell backwards again.

"You'll get used to it," said a voice from above him, and he looked up to see an elderly man with a huge ginger beard wearing a much-holed fisherman's sweater and faded cotton trousers which might once have been red, looking down at him.

"How did you get up there?" Atticus said from his sitting position on the pontoon.

"My boat's the one next door," the man said, "I heard you arrive. Obviously. Come on, I'll give you a hand. Send the bag up and then you can follow."

Atticus handed his bag up and the bearded man took it as if it weighed nothing. But Atticus, though quite a slight man, *didn't* weigh nothing. And the man looked pretty elderly. The prospect of pulling this kindly good samaritan down with him crossed Atticus's mind.

"I'm sure I can manage," he said quickly. The bearded man sighed. "It's a knack. Look." With a surprisingly light movement, he hopped over the rail of *Cangreco Loco* and landed on the pontoon next to Atticus.

"You're a friend of Salty's I take it?" he said.

"Atticus Drake," said Atticus putting out a hand.

"Francis," said the man, returning the handshake a touch reluctantly, Atticus felt. "You're not a sailor," he added, somewhat unnecessarily.

"Well spotted," said Atticus. "Salty and I were at school together. Went our separate ways. Haven't heard from him for a while actually. Call came out of the blue. Still. Great opportunity to get a bit of R and R eh?"

Francis looked at him. "That what *they* come for," he said witheringly, indicating the crowded walkway and the bustling cafes and bars across the water. "The *tourists*."

There was a bit of a silence. "You live here?" Atticus said politely. "I expect it does get a bit busy."

"I live wherever I want to," said Francis. "Last Spring I was in the Azores. Quieter. Before that, the Caribbean. May have to go back."

"Lovely," said Atticus. "Freedom. Marvellous. That's the great thing about a boat I should think. If you can actually work out how to get *on* one."

"Take hold of the stanchion," instructed Francis. "The stanchion is the vertical bit. It's the strongest. Then put one foot on the rail. Then take your weight in your shoulders, and as you reach the top, get your other foot on the rail, and move the stanchion hand much higher up. Then you can step over the rail."

Atticus watched at Francis got lightly back aboard. There was nothing for it, he would have to have a go. Taking his courage and the boat firmly in both hands he did as he had been told. The result was hardly elegant, but eventually, with a lot of huffing and puffing from him, and a fair bit of haulage from Francis, he eventually found himself on the deck of *Cangreco Loco*.

"Thanks," he said to Francis, but the faded fisherman's jersey was already back on his own boat. Francis waved but didn't look back.

Every muscle in Atticus's body hurt with the odd and sudden exertion of getting aboard. He took off his jacket and retrieved his panama hat from the deck where it had landed after the first aborted attempt to board. Salty's boat was spotless, gleaming white complemented with well-faded and scrubbed teak decking, and sunlight reflecting off the aluminium fittings. Coils of rope stood to attention on striped elastic hoops, a row of perfect knots held a row of neat blue fenders hung over the side between the *Cangreco* and Francis's boat. A bright blue canopy provided welcome shade over one half of the cockpit. The door down into the interior of the boat was unlocked, and as he navigated his way carefully inside, Atticus saw that the inside was as immaculate as the deck.

The *Cangreco*, was surprisingly spacious for a 36ft yacht. The main galley area held a fair-sized dining table which would seat at least six, and a little kitchen which was almost as well-equipped as Atticus's own back at home in London's Docklands. Through doors at the end he could see a big double cabin in the bow of the boat. Behind the stairs he found two further cabins, one of which held a fully made up bed with a note attached to one of the pillows.

Welcome aboard. Help yourself to rations, I'll be back in a bit. Salty.

Atticus put his bag on the bunk, and took off his shoes and socks. It felt surprisingly liberating to a man who was rarely seen without a decent pair of lace-ups. Padding about on the warm wooden floor deep inside the boat, he rummaged about in the many cupboards. Salty was something of a chef it seemed. All manner of herbs and spices, cooking ingredients and kitchen gadgetry was there, from a proper coffee percolator to a sugar thermometer (he made *jam*?) and a row of measuring spoons, from an extremely sophisticated corkscrew and bottle opener, to an impressive range of knives. There was even a fridge, complete with a bag of ice and half a dozen lemons in it.

Further investigation yielded a drinks cabinet underneath the galley seating, a box dedicated entirely to a case-worth of excellent red wine, and a selection of proper glasses, cleverly set into a wooden frame, prohibiting any movement when at sea.

Atticus poured himself a sizeable gin and tonic and went back up on deck, taking his book. He arranged himself comfortably in the cockpit, piling Salty's jaunty nautical cushions at his back, and began on his drink. The boat bobbed and clinked gently, and all around him, the life of the marina went on, against the sparkling backdrop of the sea and the silent heat of the mountains.

Whatever it was Salty had been thinking when he sent the invitation after all this time, it was a bit of a result. Atticus closed his eyes and breathed in the warmth and the sea air. Layers of grey English winter lifted from his shoulders and the book fell to the deck unopened, before the gin was halfway down its glass.

Chapter Five

"Well this is a fine way to greet an old mate."

Atticus opened his eyes. The sun had moved right across and was turning the sky a pale pink, as a darker shadow fell across his own face. For a moment he struggled to remember where he was and although the face which was looking down into his own was vaguely familiar he couldn't quite place it...

"Bird? *Bird*?" said the voice again, and a weathered brown hand shook him by the shoulder. "Come on old man, don't tell me you've turned into an old codger already!"

"Salty!" Atticus shouted, leaping up. The deck swam a little and he realised he was very hot. Salty's face came back into focus and he found himself looking into his friend's amused pale blue eyes. "Wow. Great to see you! How long has it been?"

Salty stepped back. "Must be fifteen years. That school reunion thing. Three hours looking at Trudy Cavanagh's legs and 24 hours worth of pub crawl."

Atticus groaned. "Sounds about right. Just before I left Cambridge wasn't it? You threatened to throw yourself in the river if Trudy Cavanagh didn't agree to marry you, and I had to tie you to a bench with your old school tie to stop you."

"Oh right, that was why you did it. Doesn't explain why you left me there though. I wasn't untied until lunchtime the next day, when two female med students jogged by and saved me."

"Ah yes, well. To tell the truth I did mean to come back for you sooner. I went round to that flat Hilly shared with those solicitor friends of hers and they laughed at me and made a fry-up to sober me up and I sort of forgot. About you. Was that really the last time we saw each other?"

"Yup. I haven't been back to Blighty since then."

"God, sorry. Surely that's not just because of the park bench thing?"

Salty said nothing. Atticus looked at him.

"*Really*?"

Salty winked. "Nope. Those med students were the business. I dated both of them in the end. Not simultaneously of course. Hung out with Mandy for a few months before she went to Australia, then took up with Candy. We were together for the best part of a year, but she started looking in jewellers' windows and taking me to other people's weddings, so I had to go. That was when I came out here. Been here, or thereabouts, since then. Nope Bird, you did me a favour when you tied me to that bench. There I was, working in pubs, messing about with riverboats and hanging out with you, and your Cambridge student mates, waiting for my adventure to start, and suddenly I realised I was missing it. That was when my life really began."

"That all seems like a long time ago," said Atticus wistfully, thinking of Cambridge and park benches. "I didn't have any idea what I wanted to do back then. Still don't. I envy you. All this," he indicated the harbour and the setting sun.

"Yeah. It is a bit good isn't it?" said Salty. A shadow crossed his face. "At least it was. I thought I had everything. Until..."

"Until what? What's happened? Salty, I've got to ask, not that it isn't great to be here, but why *did* you call me, after all this time?"

"Never mind. I'll tell you all about it later. Now, we need to go out and get suitably rat-arsed. Come along."

Salty hopped over the side of the boat onto the pontoon, just like Francis had done earlier. Atticus stood on the railing, realising that although he had eventually managed to get up onto the deck, he had no idea how to get back down again.

Salty was rummaging in a standing locker on the end of the pontoon.

"Look, the thing is," said Atticus, "I'm new to this boat thing, I'm just not sure how to...."

"Use the stairs," said Salty, dragging a small set of steps out of the locker. "That's what most people do."

It was that simple. But nobody had mentioned any steps. How was a man to know? Atticus grabbed his shoes and socks from his cabin and negotiating the steps carefully, followed Salty up the pontoon.

His friend hadn't really changed at all. Beneath his suntanned and slightly weather-beaten face, and despite the addition of a neat beard, Atticus could still see the impish, stringy kid Salty had been at St Joseph's, all those years ago.

They had teamed up early on, something to do with a mis-timed chemistry experiment and a subsequent explosion, and from then on had been pretty firm friends. Atticus had been a bookish sort of kid, eager to establish some sort of security in his life to counterbalance the somewhat eccentric circumstances at home. But he had found Salty, with his unique brand of mischief, combined with an almost superhuman ability to get away with it, irresistible. For his part, Salty had found Atticus a staunch and loyal ally in a world where he had previously been something of a loner. As soon as St Joseph's had repaired the chemistry lab, the two boys made it their unofficial headquarters, a meeting place which provided great cupboards for hiding in, a never ending supply of useful substances and equipment for practising mischief, and a sort of sentimental homage to their original alliance. Teachers and caretakers tried in vain to keep them out, and getting in became part of the excitement.

What had Salty wanted in life, back then? Just adventure. Whereas Atticus thought *he* might be an astro-physicist, or a professor of something, or even, in a particularly lovelorn phase, a poet, Salty had always answered the inevitable questions about what he planned to do with his life by saying he was just going to get away.

And get away he did. The day after the last school bell had rung at St Joseph's, as Atticus began making lists of the things he would need for his new life as a Cambridge undergraduate, Salty headed down to Poole in Dorset, picked up a crew place on a boat heading for the Caribbean, and apart from a few brief periods on land to borrow money, or fall in love, including the ill-fated Trudy Kavanagh thing, had lived afloat ever since. Atticus had received several postcards over the years, from unlikely and faraway places, always with the same message: **Gone fishing. May be some time.**

"Come on Bird, tell all. What have you been up to?" Salty had got another round in, and in the process had collected several more sailors, who pulled up chairs and looked eagerly at the newcomer.

"Me?" Atticus said.

"The thing about life on the ocean," Salty said, "Is that we're always eager to hear news from the motherland. So we can be even more sure that we've done the right thing by never going back there." The others nodded their agreement. "This is Sven," Salty indicated a tall fair haired boy. "He's never going back to Sweden. Probably because he'd be arrested. And Diego here, he's left a wife and half a dozen children in Madrid. Promises to go back, never quite gets round to it. And this is Luke, who hails from Liverpool. Enough said."

Atticus took a long drink of his extremely good and surprisingly cheap beer. "Well I can certainly see why you choose to be here rather than in England in February," he said. "I don't think I've taken my socks off in a year." He looked down at his feet, in the huge borrowed deck shoes Salty had lent him. "I don't think there's much else to report though."

"Your ma alright?" Salty asked.

"Oh yes. She's fine. I think. She's been painting again though, so you never know. Always sends her a bit, you know, off the edge. She's dressed as an American Indian at the moment. Quite a look actually. Still, it amuses the neighbours and the twins think she's awesome."

"I can imagine.The twins?"

"My sister's children. Remember Hilly? They're nearly four. Mad as their grandmother of course. Still I love them. Hilly and Hal are as lovestruck as ever, or as lovestruck as you can be with a pair of four year old mini-Hiawathas careering about the house."

"Sounds cool. You not thought about it? Marriage and kids and all that?"

Atticus had a fleeting vision of Flora. "Me? Absolutely not. Well OK, I did think about it. But it didn't work out."

"I won't ask."

"Best not to. Water under and all that. Appropriate really."Atticus indicated the harbour, still sparkling but now with the lights of the marina as the darkness drew in. "It's incredible, sitting outside at nine at night, and still being warm. I can't quite get over the fact that twelve hours ago I was shivering in the rain at Heathrow airport."

"Careful, you could end up liking it so much you won't want to leave." said Salty.

"I can absolutely see that", said Atticus accepting another drink.

Chapter Six

The thing about days which last into nights, and drink which is plentiful and cheap, and old friends with much to catch up on, is that they invariably add up to unfortunate singing. As they waved a noisy goodbye to the others and made their merry way back to the *Cangreco*, Atticus and Salty managed several choruses of *Land of Hope and Glory* before all the verses of *You Are My Sunshine* and a vaguely recognisable version of Jim Reeves' *I Love You because You Understand Me*. Whether it was due to the drink, the fact that he was already more relaxed than he had been in a decade, or whether he was taking to ocean life like a natural, Atticus had no trouble at all getting back on board, and as Salty came back up on deck with a bottle of rum and two shot glasses, he was more than ready to set sail. Salty came up beside him and took the mooring lines, reattaching them efficiently with perfect knots.

"Steady on," he said. "We'll cast off tomorrow. We have to take a tourist trip out in the morning. It'll give you a chance to get the hang of the crewing, without it being too challenging at first. Then maybe later in the week, we'll take an afternoon off, see a bit of the island. We'll have earned it by then. The toughest thing about the tourist trips is talking to the tourists."

He sat down heavily opposite Atticus and poured out generous rations of rum. Suddenly he looked very old. "Louise is brilliant at that. Talking to people. Everybody just loves her."

Atticus struggled to concentrate. This was obviously important. "Louise?"

Salty looked bleakly out across the harbour. "Louise is a truly wonderful person. You know, the sort of girl who makes everyone around her feel better. She'll do anything for anyone. We've been seeing each other for a few months. She's beautiful, I don't know what she sees in me."

"Well that's all good so far. When do I get to meet her?" Atticus asked. This *was* news, his old mate Salty, famous lone star, the one they called Desperado because he couldn't let anyone love him, had actually hooked up with a woman.

"That's just it Bird. I can't find her," Salty said sadly. "I haven't seen her for a week. Nobody knows where she is. I even went to her work, she runs a property sales company in Los Cristianos, just along the coast. Very smart offices. They haven't seen her either. They said she's probably taken off for a few days, maybe gone over to Gran Canaria or Lanzarote to see friends, or look at new properties."

"Well that sounds reasonable enough."

"But it *isn't* Bird. She wouldn't do that. Not without telling me. We had plans. We were going to spend last weekend on La Gomera, just sail over, anchor in one of the small bays, hang out with a few of our friends over there, get a bit of peace from all this," Salty indicated the party which was still in full swing in all the bars along the waterfront. "I got everything ready, cleaned the boat, stocked the gin locker, bought a few rations, and then I waited. And she didn't turn up."

"Well I'm sure there's a good reason. Have you tried calling her?"

Salty sighed."Of *course* I've tried calling her. Her mobile just rang out for a few days, and eventually it seems to have been switched off."

"Maybe she lost it. Or just ran out of battery. I shouldn't think there are many places you can charge a mobile in an emergency up in the National Park for instance."

"The National Park? Why would she be there?"

"I don't know, I'm just guessing. The Park is in all the tourist guides.I guess if I lived here, I'd go there sometimes. Maybe she just wanted a bit of time off, and found herself in the middle of nowhere?"

"That's just not Louise's style. She would always tell someone. She would probably take someone with her if she fancied a break, give someone else a treat too. That's the way she is. But either way, she wouldn't go without telling me."

"You guys are pretty serious then?"

"I think so. You know Bird, this is the first time in my life I've really thought about settling down with someone. By settling, I just mean sticking with someone. Usually around now in a relationship, around three months, I get sort of itchy feet, and then we start having arguments, and then I just leave. Untie the *Cangreco*, and sail off onto the sunset, that sort of thing. We're loners, we sailors you know. Mostly."

"But not any more?"

"Maybe not any more. Louise has changed me."

Atticus could hear the sadness in his friend's voice, but the rum was making its presence felt too, and his eyes felt heavier than ever. "Look old chum," he said, staggering to his feet. "I'm here now. Two heads are better than one. Let's talk about it in the morning. We'll have a bit of a think, and you can give me any more info you have, and we're bound to come up with a perfectly suitable explanation. Meanwhile, I'm going to turn into that extremely inviting bunk you've set up for me downstairs."

"Fair enough," said Salty, but he continued staring out into the darkness.

"We'll find her, don't you worry," said Atticus.

As he climbed into the bunk, he tried to arrange his thoughts in a way which might be some help. He hadn't liked to suggest that maybe Louise didn't feel the same way about Salty as he evidently felt about her. It was difficult seeing his old mate so unhappy. There could be any number of explanations for the girl's absence, surely? But as he tried to think, the motion of the water under the boat, and the soft hum of the music in the far distance, and the events of the day all conspired to send him into the deepest sleep he had had for a very long time.

Chapter Seven

And yet, as is so often the case when one has drunk too much and got thoroughly overexcited in general, Atticus woke up very early. At first he had no idea where he was, and was surprised to feel a gentle rocking sensation under his feet as he put them to the floor. Banging his head on the wooden ceiling reminded him that he had been sleeping in a space the size of a large cupboard, and pulling aside a tiny striped curtain, he found himself looking out of a little porthole, across the marina. People in small dinghies were already rowing themselves around, inspecting their boats at the waterline, stocking up with groceries from the shore, and repairing frayed mooring lines.

Pulling on his only pair of shorts, and a light sweater, he made his way out of the cabin and across the galley, and then climbed up and out onto the deck. The air was already warm, and the light was beautiful, a clear, flat calm light which promised another brilliant, blue-sky day.

Realising he was hungry, and with no sign of Salty, who was presumably still sleeping off the rum ration, Atticus decided to venture ashore. He would be sure to find some breakfast, every cafe and bar in the marina advertised the 'full English' and he was ready for a fry up. Unable to face the thought of socks, he borrowed an old pair of deck shoes Salty had left on deck. After a near miss with the steps which were still where they had left them, he landed a bit heavily on the pontoon, and set off, hoping he hadn't woken everyone in the marina.

Everything felt very different in the morning. It was like a little white village, The tourists had yet to arrive, and everyone was either still asleep, or getting down to work. Men in boat company uniform T-shirts hosed down the trip boats, and checked the paraphernalia of the various holiday entertainments they offered, parasailing equipment, inflatables, and jetskis. Boat owners came bleary-eyed out onto their decks and stood in their sleepwear with mugs of coffee, peacefully surveying the scenery, and counting their blessings not to be facing a grey, rainy journey to the office, or the school run.

Finding a seat outside the most Spanish-looking of the many cafes, he ordered coffee and the full works breakfast, and settled down for a pleasant hour or so. Suddenly there was an almighty crashing sound, shaking him out of his seat. Jose, who owned the optimistically named Majestic Cafe, came running out. "Oy oy *oy!*" he shouted, and issued a stream of what Atticus assumed were Spanish expletives. A small pick-up truck had dropped its cargo of huge metal barrels into the road, and its two operators were rolling them along towards the cafe.

"Always they do this," Jose explained. They throw the *bombona*, the barrels, into the street. It is easier *they* say, than lifting, and *I* say it is not so easy for my beer!"

Atticus sat down again. The morning rituals of a strange place were part of the fun of being a traveller rather than a tourist, he told himself. A thoroughly English teenager brought his breakfast, and they both surveyed the vast expanse of food. "I see the effing *bombona* men are here," she said, rather unnecessarily.

"Bit of an early morning for you?" said Atticus sympathetically.

"Not really. "I've been up all night at Veronica's. I just come straight on here afterwards."

The energy of the young, thought Atticus. He couldn't remember the last time he partied all night.

"You get a free pint of lager with that." She indicated the breakfast. Atticus looked at his watch. It was almost eight in the morning. Around him the cafe was filling up with the staff of the many tourist businesses based in the marina, ready for their breakfasts before the huge coaches arrived from the hundreds of hotels and resorts all along the South of the island. Their brightly coloured T-shirts and hoodies advertised the myriad things one could do on holiday here, Whale-watching, dolphin-spotting, game and sport fishing, jetskis and parasailing and parascending, surfing, waterski-ing, bird-watching, and some rather less healthy options, which included Foam Party Raft, Yellow Submarine, and something called Boney's Booze Crooze.

Small groups of tour operators in corporate polo shirts joined the small breakfast parties, and Atticus was pleased to note he had made the locals' choice in selecting Jose's *Majestic*. He smiled cheerfully at them. Sensing suspicion rather than camaraderie in return, he took out his phone and flicked through his emails, hoping it made him look busy and important. He deleted half a dozen spam and sales emails, before coming across one from Hilly.

"What Ho brother," she had written, **"You'll be there by now, probably sitting somewhere sunny, pretending you're a local and you've been there all your life. Remember you're nearly forty and as white as a ghost with flu, you'll stand out a mile. Wish I was there. Rain incessant, Bill and Ben incandescent, Hal in the shed."**

Atticus laughed out loud.

"Have you found Salty yet? Do give him my love. Is he still as utterly cute as ever?"

Had Hilly had a thing with Salty? Atticus couldn't remember. He had grown up being well aware of how clever and pretty, his sister was but being a brother, a boy, and younger, had never really quite worked out what was going on with the queue of embarrassed hopefuls who made their way to the door of their faded victorian house, bearing gifts and invitations to discos and the cinema. He had spent many long evenings sitting on the stairs listening to how wrong you could get this dating thing, hearing them stutter and mumble and suggest things that no girl in her right mind would ever want to do (local league football, hanging out at the shopping centre with his mates, the Imperial War Museum, stock car racing, and afternoons with Nintendo). He remembered shrugging his shoulders in sympathy as the would be suitors left, having been let down gently by Hilly.

He returned to Hilly's email:

"In an effort to make it up to myself, I'm taking the fighting Temeraires to Ma's for a few days. She's between paintings, (although still doing the Big

Chief Running Water thing according to neighbours), but I want to check she's OK, and the twins will enjoy a break. Or rather Hal will. He's on a tough case at the moment. Anyway, I'll give her your love, and let you know. Send me news of how you're getting on, and solve the mystery of why Salty has requested your presence on his lovely yacht in the sun after all this time. Tell him I'd have been far more help with whatever it is. Love you. Hx"

The remains of breakfast cleared away, Atticus found himself seriously considering the promised lager. It was only mildly alcoholic after all, and he *was* on holiday. Although he didn't know quite what was going to be expected of him. Why *had* Salty asked him to help with the missing Louise? He didn't know her, he barely knew Salty these days. He had never been here before, and his lack of local knowledge was already a source of some amusement. The waitress was regaling Sooze and Jules in full earshot of everyone in the bar, with the tale of Atticus's hilarious assumption that Veronica's was a friend at whose house she had spent the night. Veronica's was, it appeared, a notorious strip of nightclubs.

But Salty was certainly serious about Louise. The last time he'd sent one of his postcards, months ago, he had been planning to sail round the world, single handed. Was she the reason why he hadn't done it? Why he had stayed in the Canary Islands for so long? Why he had a schedule of tourist trips pinned up in the galley, to make ends meet, a man who couldn't bear to have too many people around him or anyone at all for too long? "I agree with Benjamin Franklin," he had said drunkenly last night, "Guests are like fish, they start to stink after three days."

But then he had roared with laughter and added, "Not you Bird, not you. *You* can stay as long as you like. I *need* you. I need your wise head and your real friendship. I can trust you. Not like the others."

Atticus had assumed it was the drink speaking. But now in the light of this beautiful day, a good breakfast doing its remedial work on his hangover, he began to wonder if Salty had been trying to say something more.

Bird. It was odd hearing his school nickname again. It had been Salty who invented it. "Bird after Mockingbird" he had said. "The only book I've ever read. *To Kill a Mockingbird*. And he's called Atticus, the fellow in the book. So. Atticus, Mockingbird, Bird."

And Bird, he had been to a select few, ever since.

Chapter Eight

"He was on the Heathrow inward yesterday" Sooze said to Jules, nodding in Atticus's direction as their breakfast of fresh fruit and cheese arrived. "On his *own*."

"He doesn't look like a tourist," Jules observed. "Perhaps he's an inspector from Head Office. Although if he's trying to be inconspicuous he should have gone for a bit of fake tan before he got here, he stands out like a sore thumb. Anyway, we'd better look busy just in case. How many have we got this morning?"

Sooze consulted her clipboard. "Small group for Salty, a hundred from the Taormina Princess for Whales and Dolphins, a hen party for the parascending, and a retired couple who want to ride the banana. I've given them to Mad Monty."

Jules raised his eyebrows. "They'll be fine," Sooze said sounding more confident than she felt. "Oh, and Amy's bringing those rugby boys down for a booze cruise. They're going with Diego on *Belladonna*. He should be able to manage them."

"It sounds rather as if Amy's planning on managing them," said Jules.

"So what are your plans?" asked Sooze, "once they're all off and out for a few hours? I've got to drop into the office, pick up my mail, but we could hang out up there if you want to. We don't have to be back here until after lunch."

Jules looked at his watch. "Thanks, but I've got a few things to do. I'm still not quite sorted out apartment-wise, I've been promised a two-bed in Playa Arena, but I'm still on the floor at my mate's, and it's all getting bit difficult."

Sooze looked disappointed. With Amy preoccupied with her rugby tourists, she had hoped Jules would keep her company, having been unable to decide entirely whether she fancied him or not. He had been friendly enough, especially one evening just after he arrived, when they had ended up at her place at four in the morning. Since then, she'd invited him to several events and get-togethers but he almost always found a reason why he couldn't come. Everyone came out to live in the Canary Islands for a reason, and some had more reason than others to run away from home. Perhaps he was gay. Perhaps he just didn't fancy her. He probably fancied Amy. Men always went for the obvious.

"Never mind Chica," he said, seeing her face fall, "we can hang out later if you want to. You can show me some more of the island's night life." Sooze felt only slightly better.

The marina continued to fill up and huge tourist coaches filled with hot and excited customers, keen to get out into, and onto, the sea, began to make their way down to the harbour. Atticus looked up to see Salty, bearing several large and bulging carrier bags heading towards him.

"See you've hooked up with Jose," he said cheerfully, plumping himself down on a chair next to Atticus and waving at Sooze and Jules. "We're all here it seems. Going to be a busy day."

Jose came scampering over with a mug of steaming black coffee and a basket of bread. "Senor" he said to Atticus, "I am *desolate*. I not know you are guest of Meester Salty! He is my very good friend. I bring you more breakfast."

"No No," said Atticus hurriedly. "I really couldn't eat any more. It was lovely."

"The *girl*," said Jose glaring across the terrace at the waitress. "I am apologies for her. She is a problem for me. Her mother, she *make* me employ her. She is always late, always too many parties. I suffer."

Salty laughed. "He says that about all his staff," he confided. "Now, are you ready for your first crewing experience?"

Atticus had momentarily forgotten about the sailing. It was years since he had been out on a boat, and that had been a little wooden dinghy in the Lake District. When Salty had called, he had arranged two hasty evening classes at the local comprehensive school in the hope of getting the basics covered, but had left with little more than a handbook, a head full of jargon and a new friend called Norman who had been going to the classes for years but had never actually set foot on a boat. Now it seemed Salty expected him to be useful. He wondered if he would be able to fit in a chapter of *The Lonely Sea and the Sky* before the off.

"I haven't sailed much, you know," he said to Salty, "Perhaps I could be of more help here? On land. I mean I might well be quite a liability on the boat."

"Nonsense," said Salty, "You'll pick it up. Good people always do. I've noticed that. Anyway, we have beer, we have pineapples, we have bread and ham and cheese, and we have a brisk wind out there to help us." He leant over to Jules and Sooze "Who've we got?" he asked, "Tell me the worst."

Sooze came over to the table with her clipboard. "The Whites, they're a family of five, youngest is about five I think, and a Mrs Brookes-Turnbull and her two daughters. There's a young couple too, but the last time I saw them they weren't sure if they were going to come or not. She was keen but he wasn't. Or was it the other way round? Anyway, they'll all be here in about half an hour, I've booked a couple of taxis for them, so you'd better get round there."

"Fair enough," said Salty, picking up the bags. "Sooze, this is Bird. He's my new First Mate. Come on Bird, action stations."

Atticus put a handful of Euros down on the table and followed, marvelling at Salty's constitution. They were the same age, and had drunk the same amount last night, yet Salty seemed to have suffered no ill-effects, and he was carrying those heavy bags as if they weighed nothing at all. Atticus felt old and unfit and generally useless. He was sure the suntanned tour guides and holiday reps were laughing at his little white legs, in his slightly-too-big, and certainly old-fashioned, shorts. He hoped his mission here would become apparent soon.

Round at the boat, Salty hopped aboard lightly, and began stowing the shopping in lockers, tidying up as he went. For a big man, he was exceptionally neat about everything he did. Atticus assumed it came from living with very few possessions in a very small space. Already his own cabin looked like the reject table at the end of a village hall jumble sale. He suddenly understood the real meaning of the phrase 'shipshape'.

"Last coffee before the off," said Salty, emerging from the galley with two large cups and handing one to Atticus.

"Hilly sent her love," said Atticus. "I got an email this morning."

"Ah, the *divine* Hilly," said Salty fondly.

"Tell me - did you and she.....?" Atticus raised an eyebrow.

"I am sworn to secrecy," said Salty "A sailor never kisses and tells." There was a silence and a bleak look crossed his face.

"Louise?" said Atticus. "I'm sure she'll turn up, or get in touch."

Salty turned to him. "That's why I called you," he said. "I thought to myself, who can I trust? Who's the smartest most decent man I know. That's you."

"Thanks," said Atticus, "Although I don't really think of myself as smart. But..."

Salty cut him off. "And also I could be pretty sure you weren't doing anything else. Look, the thing is, I want *you* to find her!" he said. "I want you to find Louise."

"Ahoy there!" said a loud voice, and both men turned to see a fat red-faced man in a heavy-metal band T-shirt thundering down the pontoon, followed by an equally red-faced woman bursting out of a strapless cotton dress, and three children, one head down over a mobile, one already untying mooring lines holding the other boats to their moorings, and a third swinging from his mother's shoulders as she tried to wriggle free.

"This the Cangrecky Locko?" shouted the man. "We're with you today. Permission to come aboard? Come on Shell, this is the Cangrecky Locko. I *told* her, I said, I *told* her not to bring all that stuff, why did you bring all that stuff Shell, we don't need it, I said. I *told* her we won't be needing any of that!"

Chapter Nine

"A few rules," said Salty quietly twenty minutes later, as the day's guests arranged themselves round the cockpit. Barry and Shell had already bagged the best seats, piling the cushions round them. Five year-old Tyne was mercifully asleep on his mother's lap, whilst Roger fiddled with anything he could get his hands on, enduring slaps at regular intervals from one or other of his parents. Bex continued to concentrate on her phone, texting at great speed with both thumbs. Beside Barry, slightly too close for her comfort, judging by the look of distaste on her face, was Imogen Brookes-Turnbull, a thirty-eight year old divorcee and would-be interior designer from Bath, and beside her, were her two daughters, Perdita and Lola, at seventeen and nineteen already carbon copies of their mother, in matching striped boating tops and equally matching looks of general disdain.

The final customer was Rob, a thin pale man of about twenty eight with a goatee beard and already-receding hair. Rob had a haunted look about him, and as he sweated under the mid-morning sun and the vaguely interested gazes of Perdita, Lola, Imogen and occasionally Bex, he was clearly beginning to wish he hadn't come. But then again, when he thought of why he *had* come, and what would have happened if he hadn't....

"The captain's word is final," said Salty. "I don't give many orders, I do the sailing, ably abetted by my crew..."

Atticus looked round for the crew before realising he was it.

"Anybody under fifteen or of a nervous disposition wears a lifejacket at all times," Salty continued, looking pointedly at Roger, who was already wriggling out of his. "If any of you would like to learn anything about the boat or about how to sail, let me know, and I'll show you how to you join in. Otherwise, please don't play with any of the string." Here he indicated the large number of individual ropes and lines which threaded their way round the deck. "Please don't open any of the lockers, because you may fall in, or something may fall out and kill you. Please don't run, or jump or climb on the rigging, or *I* will kill you, and if you feel sick, please do not go downstairs. You will feel worse, and it's much easier to hose you down than it is to clean up down there."

"Gross," said Bex not looking up from her phone.

"Barry'll chuck up whatever, won't you Barry?" said Shell cheerfully. "Barry only has to look at a boat and he's puking, aren't you Barry?"

"Oh *good.*" said Salty. "So glad you decided to come along anyway."

Perdita had her hand up. "If we've done like *loads* of sailing, we can take turns right?" she asked, "I mean, we usually spend our summers in the Med with Dad, and we spent Christmas in Antigua, so this will probably be a bit easy for us."

Imogen, who had not spent a summer in the Med since the divorce, and who had spent Christmas staving off floods in her rented farmhouse in Somerset looked mildly depressed.

"Actually," said Salty, "You may well find the sailing here a bit more challenging than the Mediterranean or the Caribbean. As it happens, there is an area out there, between the islands known as the Wind Acceleration Zone, or Waz, as some of the locals call it."

"Waz! Waz!" shouted Roger, snorting with laughter, "That's well rude. That means wee. Waz *Waz*.!"

Shell looked at him with something approaching pride.

"It means," said Salty after a moment, "that just as you think you're in for a peaceful potter round the coast, you may find yourself at 45 degrees trying to put two reefs in."

Perdita looked blankly at him. "Reefs," said Salty again, " But I expect you'll be fine with that won't you? With all *your* sailing experience."

He began to move round the deck, untying fenders and taking the sail cover off. Atticus felt he should be helping but he didn't quite know what to do. Then Salty started the boat's engine.

"Can you chuck the bow line onto the pontoon?" he asked Atticus.

"I have no idea," said Atticus.

Salty laughed. "Just pop up to the front, untie the rope which is attaching the nose to the jetty, and make sure it goes onto the land not into the water. Then I can reverse out. It's like taking a transit van out of a small car park really."

Atticus made his way unsteadily to the front of the boat. "You new to this?" said Rob as he passed, "You look about as shit scared as I feel."

"Oh no," said Atticus, "I've done loads of sailing. Just a bit out of practice."

"Right." said Rob, sounding unconvinced.

Atticus managed to drop the rope onto the pontoon without incident and with a bit of chugging and churning up of water, the boat moved out of its parking place and headed towards the entrance to the harbour. On the dock Jules and Sooze stood waving cheerfully, the relief at seeing their charges off for a few hours clearly evident on their well-behaved faces. A handful of people had made their way to the far end of the harbour wall and watched them chugging past.

"Bet they wish they were us," said Shell loudly. "Don't you think Barry? don't you think they're *well jell* of us on our posh boat?"

"Yeah whatever," said Barry, who was already feeling a bit green.

"Is this your boat?" Lola asked Salty, batting her eyelashes. "It's really lovely."

"Leave the man alone," snapped Imogen. Turning to Salty she put a hand on his arm. "Teenagers," she sighed, "They can be such a handful can't they?" She looked as though she was keen to get a handful of Salty.

Atticus had been dreading the moment when they actually put to sea. He felt sure he would be sick, fall over, drop something important and expensive overboard, or just generally get in the way. These smart girls with their sailing experience would run rings round him. Barry was twice his size and could probably be relied on to do anything which involved muscle. So that left him with the children and the weedy Rob as mere passengers, people who would have to be allowed for, *worked round.*

But what Atticus hadn't reckoned on, was the sea. Salty pointed the boat towards the horizon, and as they rounded the harbour wall, the current swept them up and sideways into the waves. Then he boosted the engine to take them further out, and Atticus could feel the ocean trying to take over. The wind caught him by surprise and he turned to see Salty at the helm, his hair standing on end, his face to the sun, the happiest man in the world.

Atticus clung onto the mast, relaxed his knees and found that he no longer felt as though he was going to fall over. He looked out to sea and realised that it was just amazingly, utterly, hugely, beautiful.

Chapter Ten

"He'll sort himself out in a minute," Shell said, as Barry leant noisily over the side.

"Yuk Yuk, Dad's *barfing*!" shouted Tyne, who had just woken up and was banging his father on the back with surprising force.

"Yeah, 'coz of *you* you disgusting little creep," said Bex, who still hadn't looked up from her phone but was managing the occasional sideways glance though her curtain of lank black hair at Rob, who was staring into the middle distance.

"Right," said Salty after about five minutes steady motoring, "Let's get the sail up! You girls want to do it?"

Perdita and Lola looked very scared. "Right," said Salty. "Later perhaps."

He gestured to Atticus who took over the helm, his knuckles white with the effort of holding onto the vast wheel and trying to look like a natural.

"Keep her steady, in a straight line," instructed Salty, as he scampered over the top of the yacht's cabin, and started opening latches and pulling ropes. Barry, galvanised back into the real world by the sight of activity, found himself at the business end of a winch, and together they began to raise the main sail. Atticus felt the boat pull against him as the wind filled the sail, and the two smallest children fell across the cockpit as the boat leant over into its 45-degree sailing position.

"Fuck!" shouted Shell, bracing herself against anything she could find, which happened to be Imogen. Imogen recoiled.

"Lighten up Mum," shouted Lola, who hadn't forgiven her mother for the earlier slight in front of Salty, "She's just another Mum. She's just like you!"

Somehow, and surprising themselves, each member of the crew managed to find a place to be, and as *Cangreco Loco* took to the wind, she increased her speed. None of them noticed, that on his way back to the steering position, Salty had turned off the engine. "That's it," he said to Atticus. "It's just the sea and the wind. You see?"

"Oh *yes*" said Atticus, breathlessly, as he saw.

Just as the sea beneath them moved and shifted, the rest of the world seemed to be flowing around them. Atticus felt as though he had never been on land It was as though the place where the sea met the sky was entirely within reach and he wanted to go on sailing towards it forever. He was vaguely aware of the others on the boat, but they were all lost in their own worlds and he certainly didn't want to know what those worlds were about, lest they should interfere with his own. However, after a couple of hours tacking about, using the sail to increase and decrease speed and change directions, Salty indicated that it was time to head inshore. Lola and Perdita, who had moments ago been rushing about on deck, laughing and ducking and winding winches and singing like small children, became self-conscious teenagers again as the wind died down in the lee of the land and they headed into a small bay. Stripping off to their bikinis they arranged themselves on the deck, as Salty rolled the sail away and started the engine, so he could control the boat's journey into shallower water where they could drop an anchor.

Imogen, who had been sitting on the foredeck hugging her knees and experiencing the freedom of not having to compete or judge anybody, returned to the cockpit and began fussing about suntan lotion and scarves, and Shell who had been clinging on to her bench seat for dear life, felt able to let go and follow the girls' example, taking her top off to reveal a pair of substantial breasts in an insubstantial bikini top.

"Fuck's sake woman," said Barry without enthusiasm.

"What's happening now?" Rob asked Atticus, "We're not going back are we?"

"I hope not," said Atticus, "This is about the most marvellous thing I've ever done in my life"

"You're not married then?" said Rob.

Atticus had one of his fleeting visions of Flora. "No," he said.

"Because if you were, you'd say *that* was the best thing you'd ever done in your life, wouldn't you?"

"Well I suppose it would be up there," agreed Atticus.

"But then if you *were* married, you wouldn't be doing this," said Rob

"Well, I don't know....." said Atticus.

"I do," said Rob, "If you were married, you wouldn't be doing anything *you* wanted to do. You'd just be doing things your *wife* wanted to do. Whether you wanted to do them or not. I mean, look at *them*."

He nodded at Barry and Shell who were arguing about who had put what suncream on which child and why Barry never took responsibility for the fact that their children would probably get skin cancer and it would be his fault.

"I guess, it depends on finding the right person to marry," said Atticus. Flora seemed a long way away and a long time ago.

"Now up there," Salty was saying to Imogen, who was hanging onto his every word, "you will see in the hills, the *Gran Hotel Bahia Del Duque*. Built by a sultan, in the style of a Moorish palace, it's the most exclusive hotel on the island. If you have enough cash, you can stay in the Penthouse suite, which comes with its own butler."

"Wow!" said Shell, "Look at that. Barry? Look at *that!* I'd like to stay there. Barry? I said *I'd* like to stay there! I could certainly find plenty for a butler to do for me, couldn't I Barry?"

"He could look after the bloody kids, that's what I'd like," grumbled Barry, as Atticus reassembled Tyne's lifejacket for the third time.

"*God* mum, look at that," said Perdita, who hadn't heard the conversation, "How vulgar is that building up there?" She pointed up at the hotel. "Why *are* we here? I mean, in the *Canary Islands*.

Tenerife for God's sake! *Lindsay's* family have taken her to Dubai!"

"Yes, well *Lindsay's* father didn't run away with his twenty-year-old *PR manager,*" said Imogen under her breath.

"Mum? You on about Dad and Paula *again*?" said Lola, coming to join them. "Get over it can't you? Shit happens. Can I get a drink? Do you, like, have any drinks on this?"

Salty looked at Atticus. "We'll get to the mooring," he said, "and then we'll get some *like*, drinks and maybe something to eat, and you can *like*, swim."

"Swim?" said Perdita, as if he had suggested she sweep the Aegean stables, "In the *sea*?"

"Absolutely," said Atticus. "Whales and dolphins and seaweed and all."

"*Sharks?*" shouted Roger, "Will there be sharks?"

"Of course," said Salty. "Of course there will. So you'll have to be very careful not to get *eaten.*"

"*You* wish," said Bex.

Roger looked very uncomfortable and for once was silent. "Oh, don't be pathetic!" said Lola. "Of course there aren't any sharks! He's just saying that to scare you." She didn't sound quite as certain as her words suggested.

Salty manoeuvred the boat into calm water, and dropped the anchor. Turning the engine off again, everything was quiet. They could see people on the beach, and yet they seemed as though they were in another world.

"Now here, if you look up at the cliffs, you will see dozens of little caves, set into the rock," Salty said. They all looked. "During the summer, people from all over the world come here to stay for a while. They set up house in the caves. Some of the caves are inhabited all year round."

Following Salty's outstretched hand, Atticus could make out a line of washing, rigged precariously on a ledge, many feet above them. A few metres across from it, he saw a woman, sitting in a picnic chair, reading a book, seemingly unaware that just a foot in front of her was a sheer drop.

"Blimey," said Shell. "I'd love to stay in a cave, very romantic."

"Don't be stupid," said Barry. "You couldn't stand it for a day. Look at you! Ten minutes and you'd be whining about the telly and where you were going to get your hair done!"

"Well there must be hairdressers," said Shell petulantly.

"Wow." said Rob so quietly that only Atticus heard him. "How do you get up there?"

Salty and Atticus unpacked the drinks and the bread, meat and cheese he had picked up earlier.

"Help yourselves," he said, adding apples and pineapple to the spread. Atticus opened a couple of bottles of wine and stacked the beer in a locker filled with ice.

"I want crisps," said Roger.

"He wants crisps," said Shell.

"Give him a bit of that sausage," said Barry.

"He *wants* crisps," said Shell again.

"He'll eat what he's bloody well given," said Barry. "I had to when I was 'is age. Never did me no harm."

Rob reached out a long arm and picked up a slice of cheese and a sharp knife, gripping its handle tightly. Atticus held his breath.

With a deft movement, Rob cut a small figure of a man out of the cheese slice.

"There you go," he said, handing it over to Roger. "That's a superhero that is. *Cheese Man*"

Roger looked at him in amazement, took the cheese and bit its head off.

"Cool," said Rob. "Now you're a superhero too. Only the thing is, you'll need to know, that Cheese Man hates crisps."

"I hate crisps," said Roger loudly. "Mum! I *hate* crisps!"

"Blimey," said Shell. "He's certainly taken to you. Wanna come and live with us?"

"Maybe," said Rob.

Chapter Eleven

"So," said Barry, through a mouthful of cheese and ham roll. "This boat. What's it worth?"

"Shutup Barry," said Shell. "You're always on about what things are worth. He *is*!"

"Hang on a minute and I'll tell you," said Salty, disappearing down into the galley. A moment later he came back. "Two hundred and fifty thousand pounds," he said.

"Right," said Barry. "Well, when I win the lottery."

"What?" said Imogen icily. "When you win the lottery *what?* You'll buy this boat? What would *you* do with a boat?"

"We could 'ave a boat if we wanted," said Shell, narrowing her eyes as she looked at Imogen. "You think just because we live on an estate, we couldn't 'ave a boat? Only people like you have boats right? Well I've got news for you. Barry's just got me a Mercedes. Soft top. So there. Bet *you* don't have a Mercedes soft top."

Shell turned her attention to Barry. "You could 'ave a boat if you wanted," she said, "I told her. But there are a few more of us who'll be 'aving a say in how that lottery money's spent first. Before you go throwing your money around."

"She wants one of them timeshares," Barry said aside to Atticus, " I told her, it's a *scam*. I said to her, it's all a scam, but will she listen? She will *not*."

"I used to have a timeshare," said Imogen sadly. "In Costa Rica. I suppose *she's* got it now. *Paula.*"

Atticus took a piece of cheese and a beaker of wine and headed for the foredeck. Right now he just wanted to be alone, with the sun and the sea, bobbing about, without a care in the world. A moment later Salty joined him. The two men sat in companionable silence, looking ahead at the horizon, whilst in the background, the bickering of Barry and Shell, the demands of Imogen's daughters and the mayhem Roger and Tyne were creating in the galley faded into insignificance.

"Why did you go downstairs when Barry asked you what the boat was worth?" said Atticus.

Salty laughed. "I have a chart in my cabin," he said, "I mark on it every time someone asks me what *Cangreco's* worth. For some people it's all they care about. And then I have a rota of answers. Sometimes its half a million, sometimes it's ten thousand quid. Sometimes I do it in dollars. It never makes any difference. They all say they'll buy it if they win the lottery."

"Not that you'd ever sell," said Atticus. "This is the good life, isn't it? It seems too good to be true."

"Don't say that," said Salty.

"I know," said Atticus. "But we'll find her. I'll help you. We'll get to the bottom of it."

As they finished their lunch, most of the guests decided to swim and Salty lowered a ladder off the back of the boat. Imogen, Perdita and Lola all in impressively expensive swimwear, executed neat little dives, throwing their shiny hair about as they surfaced and checking to see if anyone had noticed them. Shell, now in an optimistic floral one-piece shuffled forward on her bottom before lowering herself gingerly down the ladder, where she was almost drowned by the bow wave created by Barry leaping over her head and landing bottom-first in the water. The two smaller children followed their father's example, slightly hindered by water wings, while Bex remained on deck, taking an opportunistic selfie on her phone which made it look as though she was on an expensive yacht, alone with Salty. Rob, in a greying T-shirt and faded board shorts stood shivering at the prospect of swimming before putting his jeans back on again and finding himself a bench seat in the galley where he proceeded to fall asleep. The trouble with Liv is that she was at her most active and insistent at night, To be honest he was rather tired of sex.

Atticus was still enjoying the peace and quiet when two more boats arrived in the bay. The first was a very neat little yacht, with a bright blue hull, which slid neatly onto a mooring. At first it looked as though there was nobody at all on it, but then he saw a small blonde girl tidying the deck.

"Aha," said Salty waving. "Now we're in for a treat. You're about to meet Pookie."

"Pookie?" said Atticus, thinking 'who the hell is called *Pookie*?'

The blonde made sure her boat was secure, and throwing off her sailing jacket and very short white shorts revealing a bright red one-piece, dived into the waves and headed towards them. Imogen and the girls, late to notice the competition, followed, mouths open as she hauled herself equally neatly up onto the deck of the *Cangreco*.

"*God* Darling," the girl said shaking her well-cut hair so that drops of salt water flew in every direction, "Haven't you got any champagne on the go? I'm *gasping*. Don't tell me I'll have to go back for it?"

Salty reappeared from the galley with a bottle. "I keep it for Pookie," he explained, "She won't drink anything else. Atticus, meet Pookie, Pookie, this is my oldest mate, Bird. Atticus Drake."

Pookie looked Atticus up and down. "My," she said, "Aren't you a handsome thing?" She looked directly at him, revealing deep brown eyes which sparkled.

"I shouldn't think so," said Atticus. "Glad to meet you." He felt his heart bounce.

"Pookie," he added bravely, "Is that your real name?"

Pookie laughed. "Maybe," she said, "On the other hand, who the hell would be called Pookie?"

Atticus waited, but if he had hoped she would volunteer her real name, he was disappointed. Instead she asked, "Atticus. Is that *your* real name?"

"Yes," said Atticus. There was a silence. "I like it," she pronounced, before adding "Oh Hell!" suddenly.

She's realised I am not a handsome thing, thought Atticus, before he realised her attention had been distracted by the second newcomer to the bay. A slightly tatty boat was lurching across the water, tipped to one side and then the other by a number of very big men running about on the deck and falling over one another. They missed the mooring the first time, narrowly avoided drifting onto rocks to the right of the bay's entrance, swung round, and returned to the buoy, lassoing it at the second attempt with much cheering and yelling. One of the men appeared to fall overboard which caused even more amusement. A single girl in the uniform of the Cupcake Tour company made a futile attempt to calm them down.

"Poor Amy," said Salty, handing glasses of champagne to Pookie and Atticus, "She may just have taken on more than she can handle this time. That, I am reliably informed, is the larger portion of a minor league rugby team."

"Will she need rescuing?" Pookie asked. "I could go over and check that mooring for her."

"Let's just see how they get on," said Salty. "The bay's fairly calm, there's a limit to how much trouble they can get into."

"So you're a keen sailor then?" Atticus said to Pookie.

"You could say that," said Pookie.

"Or you *could* say that she's one of only a handful of women ever to have sailed single-handed across the Atlantic," said Salty.

"Oops," said Atticus. "Sorry. I don't know much about sailing. Except that so far I rather like it."

"Good for you," said Pookie. "I couldn't live without it." She drained the first glass of champagne and gestured to the bottle. Atticus rushed to refill her glass.

"Anyway Salts, where's that marvellous girl of yours? I was going to invite you for dinner this evening. You too of course," she added to Atticus. "She off selling overpriced mansions to people who will only visit them once in a decade?"

"There appears to be a bit of a question mark about Louise at the moment," said Atticus diplomatically. Salty seemed to have been hypnotised by the mention of Louise, and was staring ahead at where the rugby boys had all thrown themselves, fully clothed, into the sea.

"No kidding?" Pookie said, "Really? She hasn't dumped him has she? No of course she hasn't, who would? *I* certainly wouldn't. Anyway they seem so bloody perfect for each other. And I say that as a woman who has never found anyone even halfway acceptable."

"I can't believe that," said Atticus gallantly.

"Oh you'd be surprised," said Pookie. "Surprised how many men are put off by the boat, the money, of which, to spare you having to ask politely later, there is a substantial amount, or the fact that every six months or so I have to go to sea entirely on my own, just to stay sane."

Atticus wanted to say that he thought he could handle all of those things, if they were wrapped in such extremely attractive packaging, but decided against it. He felt instinctively that Pookie wasn't the kind of girl who would be impressed by gallant compliments.

"So where *is* Louise then?" Pookie said, as Salty began tidying away the remains of the lunch and tidying up the cockpit.

"We don't know," said Atticus. "Salty has asked me to come out and lend a hand in finding her. Well some moral support really I suppose. It seems she was supposed to meet him last Friday evening, ready for a weekend on some island…"

"La Gomera I expect," said Pookie. "Lovely. Very romantic. We could go over some time. Depending on how long you're staying" She looked him up and down. "But we need to get onto this Louise thing. So she didn't turn up?"

"No." Atticus tried to concentrate on Salty. "And she hasn't made contact since. Which is apparently unusual. And none of her work colleagues know where she is."

"The thing about the Canaries," said Pookie. "It may look like a paradise island for holidaymakers and indeed it is. But it's also one of those places where people go to hide themselves. Or to lose themselves. And sometimes people just want to be hidden or lost, and sometimes other people want to hide or lose someone."

"That sounds ominous," said Atticus.

"I don't want to alarm you," said Pookie. "But I know a lot of people here. And some of them aren't as nice as others."

She looked at him again, this time more searchingly, "You think you can help?"

"I don't know," said Atticus truthfully. "But I can try. Sometimes, a fresh pair of eyes and all that."

"Do you have any experience of solving mysteries?"

"Oddly enough I found myself in a bit of a scrape last year," said Atticus. "Venice."

"Venice? Very spooky."

"As it turned out, yes."

"I've got a couple of dear friends there. Lovely George of course. And Bill goes there a lot."

"Bill?"

"Nighy."

Atticus remembered how Hilly had asked him to pass on her love if he ever met Bill Nighy.

"Yes I had heard," he said.

"I'll help you all I can."

"Thanks."

"We'll start this evening. You will come won't you? I'm on Trousers 13."

"Trousers?"

"*Pantalon*. Trousers."

Atticus laughed. "Quite. Yes, we'll be there."

"Great. You can bring me some more of this," she indicated the champagne. "*Very* acceptable."

Salty had begun signalling to the customers to get back on the boat.

"Oh hell, the mob descends," said Pookie, handing him her empty glass. "I can't wait to see how that chunky bloke gets back up here. See you later!"

And before he could respond, she had done another beautiful swallow dive over the side of *Cangreco* and was gone, her swimsuit a flash of scarlet in the blue sea. He watched until he saw her climb aboard her own boat, wishing he had binoculars and then being ashamed of himself.

"Cellulite," said Imogen acidly, as she and her daughters watched Pookie's perfect body moving through the water.

"Who's your lady friend then?" said Barry loudly, dripping all over Atticus's feet.

"Barry? *Barry*?! Don't leave me!" shrieked Shell, who was having rather more trouble coming up the ladder than she had going down it, gravity not being on her side. Salty took pity on her and hauled her up with a strong arm which she held onto for rather longer than was technically necessary.

Eventually they were all back on deck, and sitting damply in the cockpit, as Salty took up the anchor and started the engine.

As they left the bay, Atticus noticed the sun glinting off something on the shore, right at the end of the rock promontory. Looking more closely, he saw a man, in an improbably long coat, given the heat and the territory, with a pair of binoculars trained on *Cangreco*. Atticus looked round to see if he was mistaken, and the source of attention was something else, an interesting seabird perhaps, or another yacht crewed by more beautiful people, but they were the only ones in direct line with the binoculars. Atticus waved, to show he had seen the man, but instead of waving back, the man promptly turned and ran along the rocks. He was surprisingly agile, especially given the coat.

"Did you see that man?" Atticus said to Salty, as they turned out of the bay and headed along the coastline.

"What man?" said Salty.

"A man in a raincoat, with a pair of binoculars. Standing there, right on the edge of the rocks. He was looking right at us!"

"Raincoat?" said Salty. "You're seeing things. It hasn't rained here for four months."

As they motored gently back along the shore, Imogen and the girls spread themselves across the deck, drying their hair and admiring their barely-there tan lines, whilst the children threw water and flicked crushed balls of bread at them. Shell shouted at them sporadically and Barry fell loudly asleep.

"See you're getting along with Pookie then," said Salty.

"Yes. well she seems very nice."

"I should warn you, she's not the settling down type."

"Yes she said that."

"Great. As long as you know."

"We're going to have dinner on her boat."

"Are we?"

Oh yes. *Definitely*."

Chapter Twelve

By the time *Cangreco* entered the harbour, Atticus felt sufficiently confident to scamper up to the foredeck ready to catch the rope which Sooze, who had spent the afternoon battling with paperwork and wishing she was in a bar with Jules, threw vaguely in his direction. "How was it?" she said to him, as the customers began to gather up their belongings.

"Great," said Atticus, happily.

"You wait until you've been here for six months," said Sooze. "You'll find the novelty wears off."

"Right," said Barry loudly, striding off up the pontoon, all thoughts of his earlier seasickness forgotten. "Where's the nearest lager?"

Shell trailed children, towels and the remains of the lunch, which she had packed into her own handbag, behind her.

"Hang on a minute," said Atticus, watching them go, "Weren't there *three* children?"

Sooze looked at Shell, who was being ignored by Bex and clambered on by Tyne. Then she looked at her clipboard.

"Roger," said Atticus.

"You've picked up the lingo pretty quickly," said Sooze.

"No. Not Roger as in Roger and out. Roger. The middle kid?"

Sooze went a bit pale under her tan.

Atticus yelled at Salty, who was winding ropes and stowing them away in the cockpit lockers, while Imogen tried to persuade him to join her for a drink at their hotel later in the evening.

"Have you got Roger?" he shouted.

Salty looked up, then round, and then shook his head. Shell, who had reached the top of the pontoon realised she was a child short and began waving her arms frantically.

"For goodness sake," said Imogen. "If these people will insist on having so many children you would think they would at least try and keep track of them."

There was a shriek from the galley, and Perdita came rapidly up the steps, followed by Lola.

"*Disgusting* child," they said in unison. Atticus, Salty and Imogen looked down into the galley where Roger, completely naked, had covered himself in what looked like sun cream. He grinned up at them.

Atticus made his way into the galley and tried to get hold of Roger, who was now slipperier than an eel. He suggested the kid might like to put his clothes back on, but that was a definite no go.

"Come on old sport," he said eventually. "You can't stay here, your mum will be wondering where you are....Look, I'll give you a fiver." Roger nodded happily and put out a hand.

"That lotion costs £45 a bottle!" wailed Lola. "It's only available in Harvey Nichols!"

Atticus tried to grab an arm, but Roger slipped away and shot up the steps onto the deck. Imogen screamed and stepped back to avoid coming into contact with him, landing in an ungainly fashion on the deck with her legs in the air.

"Bloody hell Mum," said Perdita chillingly. "Get a grip."

There was a great rocking and sloshing of water and Barry reappeared on the pontoon.

"Get down here you little bastard or I'll 'ave yer!" he shouted. The occupants of several other yachts stopped their hosing and polishing and looked up. Roger stopped. For a moment it seemed as though he was going to defy his father, but suddenly he thought better of it. Grabbing him by a hand, Barry hauled the child through the guardrails of the boat as though he weighed nothing and dumped him on the pontoon. Atticus handed the child's clothes down.

"Little bugger," said Barry, 'Takes after his mother."

Imogen had pulled herself together and was also leaving. "So," she purred to Salty. "I'll see you later shall I?"

Perdita and Lola climbed down after her. "You paid 45 quid for sun cream?" said Perdita.

"It isn't suncream," hissed Lola. "It's quick-action fake tan."

Some way in the distance, the red-faced Barry, the red-shouldered Shell, the ghostly Bex, the vaguely grubby Tyne and the already-darker Roger squabbled their way back to the tour bus.

"Thanks for the trip," said Rob, who had reappeared while nobody noticed. "That was cool."

Salty smiled and shook his hand. "Glad you enjoyed it. You out here on your own?"

Rob smiled weakly. "Girlfriend. Her idea actually. She's waiting for me back at our hotel. She wanted to come on the boat but I said *I'd* stay behind. Fancied a walk and a quiet beer actually. Then at the last minute she said she'd stay with me. So I got on the bus. Now I have to go back and tell her why I did it."

"Why *did* you do it?"

"Don't know really. Just wanted to get away. You know."

"Oh yes," said Salty. "I know. You can come again if you like, later in the week. No charge."

"I won't be allowed," said Rob. "But thanks anyway."

He got off the boat and wandered slowly up behind the others. Sooze and Jules could be seen in the distance, waving at him to hurry up.

A couple of hours passed peacefully with Salty and Atticus spending time cleaning up the boat and repairing anything which Shell's children had damaged. Salty seemed to take pride in his work, restoring his kingdom to its former pristine glory, and Atticus just loved being on board, with the blue of the sea all round him, the gentle rocking of the boat, and the lovely way that all sound was slightly muffled by the water. It was like being on a cloud, lifted just above the seething mass of humanity, so you could see and hear and feel everything that was going on, without having to deal with any of it. Salty had heaved a huge sigh of relief as they noticed Sooze and Jules' tour bus exiting the port and heading away up the hill.

"You must hate all these tourists lumbering about on *Cangreco*," said Atticus, as they swabbed the remains of Lola's fake tan from the wooden galley floor.

"I don't mind actually," said Salty. "I mean I don't love all of them obviously. But it means I get to keep the boat here, and it pays for the drinks. And sometimes you meet people who really need it, you know."

"Like that Rob?"

"Yup. There's a man who will spend his whole life in some grey bit of England, working in some dreary dead-end job, married to some dull girl, and all the time, he could be out there, seeing the world. For some people, the dead-end thing is all they want. They come out here or somewhere like this, once a year, and it's lovely and hot and sunny and everyone's nice to them, and for a moment they think they want to live like this. But the truth is by the end of a fortnight, they're glad to get home. But every now and then, you see something, someone else. And you just hope you've done enough to show them that life doesn't have to be dreary. That they are in control of their own destiny. That there are choices."

"Blimey," said Atticus, "That's a lot to deal with. Not sure Rob's quite up to it."

"No. You may be right" said Salty. "Look, I thought I'd go up to Los Cristianos again in a bit. See if Louise has been in touch with her office. You never know. You coming?"

"Why not?" said Atticus.

"You'll like the town," Salty said. "It's more real than a lot of the island. It's still a fishing port. Real people live there."

What Atticus thought he *would* like, was a good look at Louise's work colleagues. Maybe there would be a clue as to where she was.

"I'll get some shoes," he said.

Chapter Thirteen

"I don't own it," Salty said as they chugged up the steep hill from the marina and turned onto the motorway in a very battered red Renault 5. "I rent it. We all rent our cars here."

Atticus wondered if it was rented, why Salty didn't consider renting something a bit less battered, but he didn't ask. The little car continued valiantly along, overtaken by trucks and lorries and the ubiquitous Mercedes' taxis, all hooting and emitting clouds of diesel, but Salty seemed unperturbed.

After about ten miles they turned off the motorway and headed down towards the sea again, this time finding themselves in a biggish town, spread out on many levels, all facing the ocean. At the bottom, a wide harbour was filled with a number of much more serious looking fishing boats, together with warehouses, cranes, and the necessary industrial equipment for the trade. Salty found a parking space and stopped. They got out and turned uphill until they came to a small parade of shops and bars.

"I keep thinking she's here," he said. "That I'll just go into the office and there she'll be."

"Perhaps she will," said Atticus.

But they could tell as they went in that she wasn't. The office of Paradise Property was small and modern, one of a row of matching glass-fronted offices, with brightly lit interiors and pictures of beautiful modern villas and swimming pools to entice would-be property buyers and holidaymakers who were serious about wanting to stay. And serious they would have to be, Louise Renton dealt only in the smartest and most expensive of the island's apartments and villas.

As they made their way towards the office, Salty filled Atticus in on Louise's road to success. She like many others, had originally come out to Tenerife on holiday, as a treat after finishing her university degree in property management. Loving the sunshine and sensing a gap in the market, she had started by acting as go-between for another of the island's property dealers, showing clients round properties and opening negotiations before she plucked up the courage to set up on her own. Now, just three years later, she employed a small team and had already made quite a name for herself. She had met Salty when she hired *Cangreco* for a corporate team-building trip.

"So, the man she worked for, was he supportive when she left to set up in competition?" Atticus asked.

"He couldn't really object," said Salty. "He was in jail. Turned out he'd been mixed up in some shady developments in the North of the island. The authorities here and in the UK had been after him for years. Luckily they believed Louise when she said she had no idea."

"Right," said Atticus, filing away the information.

"Oh it wasn't like that," said Salty, seeing his look. "She's as honest as the day's long. I know it."

"Of course," said Atticus.

"This is Marge," Salty said, opening the door of the office and heading towards a thin girl sitting at a desk, filing her cerise-painted nails. "She's the receptionist. Everything starts with Marge and if she doesn't know you, you haven't been here!"

The girl waved cheerily, causing her many bangles to rattle and the ringleted curls on her head to bob up and down. "And before you ask," she said in a high-pitched Lancashire-accented voice, "She's not been in, not since the last time you asked. And I'd like to know what's goin' on, I'm supposed to go back to the UK next week for me nan's ninetieth."

A young man in a shiny suit came into the reception area from a back office. "Wotcher," he said to Salty. "Hey Marg*areeen?* You want to know how great I am? I. Am. *Epic.* You hear me?" He playfully slapped the back of Marge's head, really quite hard.

"This is Darius," said Marge, a grim look on her face "More prick than epic if you ask me."

"Marge? You don't mean it! You love me really. I've just sold Bougainvillea Villa, for nearly nine hundred Ks! After just *two weeks!*" said Darius, attempting unsuccessfully to kiss her on the cheek.

"Get off," she said, without looking up from her work. "You 'aven't seen anything of Louise have you?"

"Louise?" said Darius, as if it was the first time he'd heard her name. "I have not." Was it Atticus's overactive imagination, or did he look a bit shifty?

"Why, she still not called in?" Darius made a big deal out of fussing about with a file he was carrying.

"Bet she's off with some rich buyer, looking at *properties*."

He put the file down and did that irritating thing of putting his fingers up in little quotation marks, to indicate he meant that Louise might be looking at something which definitely wasn't properties.

"Don't be an arse," said Marge, nodding at Salty.

"Sorry mate. No offence," Darius said, realising too late who Salty was.

"Hi Marge," said Atticus. "I'm Atticus."

Darius made a snorting noise and disappeared back into the office.

"Don't take any notice," Marge said. "Darius is a tosser. But he can certainly sell houses." She picked up the file which Darius had left and put it in her in-tray. "I'll be here late now, processing that. Still, nine hundred. Some people really do have it all."

"Marge, when was the last time you saw Louise?" Atticus asked.

Marge looked up. "Everyone asks me that," she said. "It was Thursday. I was off early because it was me mate's birthday and we was going round hers to get done up before heading off to Veronicas. That's ....."

"I know, nightclubs," said Atticus.

"Right. And Louise came in and said she was off for the weekend, going on the boat with, well, with *him*, and could I cover Saturday morning? So I said

I could and she said that was fine, and she would see me on Monday."

"And that's all?"

"Yup. I already told Salty." Salty nodded and turned to go. "Thanks Marge," he said sadly. "You'll let me know if you hear from her?"

"Although..." Atticus turned back as Marge continued.

"Yes?" he said.

"Well it was very late. Or really it was early. Friday morning. We was comin' back from the strip. That was a night. Mind you Shanae can drink, I'll give 'er that. I can 'ardly keep up. We walked right past here. Well, across the end of the Parade there, by the Irish bar. And I thought I saw a light on. In the office like. So I says to Shanae, I'll go an' check and she says not to bother. But just as I was going to come down here anyway, although I didn't really want to, me shoes was killing me, I saw this man, come out. He went the other way, and the light wasn't on any more, so I went home and didn't think any more of it."

"But it was unusual for anyone to be in the office at that time?"

"We open at eleven. That's why I like the job really. I'm not much of a morning person."

"And this was earlier than that?"

"Yeah, I said. It was probably about six. Veronica's turns out about then, so they can wash all the floors and seats down and everyone can go and get some sleep."

"Sounds lovely. You didn't recognise the man?"

"Nah. But I was a bit drunk. Probably. Not that I get drunk a lot you know. Shanae's a bad influence on me. But it wasn't Salty for definite.This guy was wearing a coat. Not much call for a coat here."

"What sort of coat?"

"I don't know!" Marge was beginning to sound impatient. "Look it was just a coat. One of them long beige things. The ones with the checked insides the Japanese people like so much. Expensive. But he was a long way off."

Atticus could see Salty pacing up and down the parade outside the shop. "You mean a raincoat?" he said. "Look, I'd better go. You will let us know if you hear anything won't you? He's very worried."

"He's nice, that Salty. She's lucky to 'ave him I reckon" said Marge. "I would. You know. If she doesn't come back. You could put a word in?"

"Thank you for that," said Atticus.

"I just thought..." said Salty as they headed back towards the harbour a minute later.

"I know old man," said Atticus. "Come on, there must be somewhere we can get a drink round here."

Chapter Fourteen

They headed back downhill towards the waterside and settled themselves on red plastic chairs under a striped awning, ordering *cafe cortado*, which clearly annoyed the waiter who had cleaned the machine down after the day and was planning on opening up the bar. They were the only customers, except for a single man hidden behind a newspaper. Atticus noticed long tanned legs in very nice and probably expensive deck shoes protruding from under *El Pais*. A local then, rather than a tourist.

"Tell me about her," said Atticus, since there was clearly no point in trying to talk to Salty about anything else.

Salty pulled his phone out of his shorts pocket and found some photographs on it. In the first, a very pretty woman with shiny chestnut hair tied in a ponytail smiled into the camera, her back to the coastline Atticus had seen that morning.

"That's on the boat right?" he said. Salty nodded.

"The first time we went out." he said, scanning through more photographs and then back again. "She was a natural sailor. This next one was taken by one of the punters, a bit later. We'd just got back to the harbour and he suggested taking it as he got off. I remember thinking it was a nice thing, to think of it. Most people don't bother about the staff, they just take pictures of each other."

The second shot was of Salty and Louise, standing on the deck of *Cangreco,* with the harbour behind them. Both were wearing sunglasses, so you couldn't see their eyes. Salty was looking at the camera, Louise was looking at Salty. At first glance there was nothing else to see, just two people clearly fond of each other, on a day out. But as he looked more closely, Atticus thought he could see something else. In the reflection of Salty's sunglasses, he could just make out part of the reflection of the person taking the picture. The face was obscured by the camera, but it was the legs which gave it away. Those long tanned man's legs, in those particular deck shoes.

Atticus turned round, but they were alone in the cafe.

"Just a customer, you say?" he asked.

"Yup. He'd been out with us for one of our morning sail and swim trips. He was with a couple of others I think, although I can't actually remember. It was quite a busy morning. He didn't swim though, I definitely remember that, because he was chatting to Pookie in the bay. I thought she might have made a date with him actually, but she hasn't mentioned it since. Anyway I remember especially that he didn't ask how much the boat was worth. So that makes him a good guy."

"Well," said Atticus carefully. "It's a lovely picture."

Perhaps he was mistaken. Perhaps he just had legs on the brain, with his own being so colourless and unsexy. Perhaps he should invest in some fake tan. Or some expensive deck shoes. He would certainly change into trousers before Pookie's dinner party this evening.

"*She's* lovely" said Salty looking longingly at the picture before putting the phone away.

Across the harbour they saw a sunburnt woman shouting instructions at a small dark-skinned child who was trying to scale a rusting ladder used by fishermen to haul their catch up onto the dock at low tides. Moments later there was a splash.

"Roger," said Salty. "He's gone in."

"He's out again." said Atticus a moment later, as a couple of teenage boys dived into the harbour to haul him back onto land.

They paid their bill, and, stopping at the supermarket to pick up a couple of bottles of champagne for Pookie, they headed back to the car.

Chapter Fifteen

Atticus tried on both the pairs of trousers he had brought with him, deciding jeans looked too English and touristy, and linen looked too PG Wodehouse, before deciding that Bertie Wooster was preferable to *Top Gear* and adding a blue cotton shirt.

"Cool," said Salty as Atticus appeared back on deck. "That should work. Pookie likes an English gent."

"I wasn't trying... I mean, I haven't really *got* anything else," Atticus protested but Salty was laughing, Even he had made an effort, and had showered and neatened up his beard before putting his slightly smarter shorts on. Pookie obviously expected some effort to be made, and Atticus was glad he had bothered. They collected the champagne and walked round the harbour to where Pookie's pretty blue yacht was moored. The evening was just beginning, and Atticus revelled once again in the warmth and the lights on the sea, and the lovely relaxed atmosphere of the many bars and restaurants. He could smell grilled fish and chicken, and the indefinable scent of the sea in a hot country.

"You wait," said Salty, "It's Friday. Karaoke night. By ten thirty a hairdresser from Manchester will be sobbing her way through *I will Survive*, before Barry from Wolverhampton gives us his unmistakeable rendition of *My Way* and those rugby boys of Amy's will have a go at *Bohemian Rhapsody*. Hardly traditional Canarian culture."

"Or perhaps it is," said Atticus. "Where would you go if you *did* want some authentic local food and music?"

"I'd head for the hills," said Salty. Adeje, is a lovely town, lots of great bars and restaurants. They've all got their house specialities. We go up there when we can, to eat *pollo al ajillo*, at Casa Miranda, or if it's a real celebration, we go to Acosta's for the *solomillo al pimiento*. If you head along the coast beyond the tourist routes, there are a good few fishing villages where you can hang out with locals too, eat seafood you've just seen pulled out of the sea. Ideally, we'd go over to La Gomera or La Palma. We'll do it, if you're here long enough and if....."

"*When* Louise comes back," Atticus said confidently.

Pookie was standing on the deck of her boat, the *Grace Kelly*. She was wearing a bright orange cocktail dress and brandishing glasses already filled with champagne as they arrived. "Welcome darlings!" she said. "How many of us?" she whispered to Atticus as he used her very comfortable plank to walk from the pontoon onto the deck. Why didn't Salty have a proper gangplank?

"Just two," Atticus whispered back, noticing Pookie's scent as he got close to her. It was like the sea, blue and airy, with a background hint of something flowery.

"Ah," she said. "Never mind. We will bring out the big guns and make this a party to help us get through our Troubles."

Atticus, unable to resist sharing his new glamorous life, took a picture of Pookie, Salty and the champagne and emailed it to Hilly.

It's all very hard work, he wrote. **Wish you were here?**

On the shore behind them, a gang of huge and very drunk Englishmen began a darts tournament. Amy had been joined by Jules and Sooze who had the evening off and had been drafted in to help, although Jules was showing very little inclination to be only use at all, lounging at the far end of the bar with a beer and chatting up a waitress.

"How's it going?" Amy tried to whisper above the racket as one of the boys began with a double top which seemed to involve a round of tequila slammers. She nodded in the direction of Jules. Sooze made a face. "Not as good as I'd hoped to be honest. He just doesn't seem to be picking up my vibes."

"Maybe you're being a bit subtle?" Amy suggested, with a slight thrust of her bottom lip and a flick of her bouncy hair. "Sometimes you have to show them what you've got."

"That rather depends on what you have got," said Sooze gloomily, looking over Amy's tanned cleavage. "I asked him if he wanted to stay at my apartment for a while, if his doesn't work out and he said No."

"Well that certainly rules subtle out," Amy said. "Bit soon to suggest it perhaps? Maybe you should have waited until he was desperate?"

"Thanks a lot!" said Sooze.

"All I can say is, if you're short of male company you've come to the right place."

A bad shot missed the board and hit the chalk wall menu between egg and chips and the paella specials. Another round of tequila slammers was ordered.

"Well there are plenty to go round," Sooze admitted. "Any out of bounds?"

"Not so as you'd know," Amy said. "Most of them are married, but that hasn't stopped at least three of them staying out, or *in,* somewhere than wasn't their hotel. I like Gary, he's the one on the left. He's promised to take me to Little Italy one evening. But the rest are all yours."

Sooze looked over to where Jules was sitting, seemingly oblivious to everyone else.

"Do you think he might be....?" Amy said.

"I really don't know," said Sooze. "He doesn't seem to be, well, *anything.*"

Amy put a hand on her arm. "Come on," she said. "This is the best party in town. Let's enjoy it."

"Actually," said Sooze, "*That's* the best party in town. But we aren't invited."

They looked over to the *Grace Kelly,* where Atticus, Pookie and Salty were drinking champagne and making a start on Pookie's excellent selection of beautiful Canarian canapes.

"Did you make these?" Atticus asked politely.

Pookie winked. "Do I look like the kind of girl who spends her afternoons knocking up canapes?" she laughed. "I *have* someone."

"Pookie always has someone," said Salty.

"I was scuba diving in Garachico this afternoon," she said cheerfully. "Spectacular water."

It was a lovely evening. Pookie proved to be very diverting company, and Salty became almost cheerful under the influence of her many hilarious anecdotes and the free-flowing champagne. The canapes gave way to an excellent seafood dinner, which they ate by candlelight on the deck, to the increasingly mad accompaniment of the rugby boys' darts tournament and the early strains of karaoke from McSweeney's bar further along the strip. Atticus could hardly believe how quickly the time had passed when Salty announced it was midnight.

"How do you know?" said Atticus, Salty hadn't looked at a watch or a phone.

""Whitney Houston," said Salty, as an immense wailing sound filled the air. "She does *I will always love you* on the dot of midnight. Not the real Whitney Houston obviously. Although I can believe this noise comes from beyond the grave."

Atticus stood up, a little unsteadily. As he looked out over the harbour a cold shiver ran down his spine. "Salty," he said, "Is there someone on your boat?"

Salty and Pookie put down their glasses and looked over to where *Cangreco* was moored. A small moving light was darting about the deck, disappeared, and a moment later reappeared in the porthole window of Atticus's cabin. Then it went out altogether and it took their eyes a moment to get accustomed to the darkness. Pookie came up from her own galley with a pair of binoculars and handed them to Atticus.

A dark shadow was still moving about on *Cangreco*.

Chapter Sixteen

At six that evening, Hilly, tired, and weary after over two hundred miles' driving, mostly in the rain, from Cambridge to Devon, with only five stops for drinks, wees, the retrieval of missing wooly companions which had fallen into footwells, checking of pockets and luggage for further wooly companions who could not be left behind, the replaying of lengthy story tapes and one throwing up incident, pulled into the driveway of her mother's crumbling old victorian home. Behind her, after seven hours' non-stop excitement at going to see Granny Cake, the twins had just, and only just, fallen asleep.

"Darling!"

Acclaimed artist Rebecca Flint Drake, resplendent in multicoloured linen layers and an authentic indian headdress came out to greet them. "Thank *goodness* you're here. Now we can break out the gin."

Hilly, who could think of nothing she wanted more, wondered whether she could legitimately ask if they could have drinks in the car, to save waking Bill and Ben. The rain intensified, and it was almost dark, although given the grim English February weather, the light had barely changed since lunchtime.

"Hi Ma," she said. "I wish you lived in Italy. Or Spain. Or the Caribbean."

"So do I darling," said Rebecca. "But I don't. I live here. And anyway if I did, how would you get my beloved heirs to me?"

"I'd *post them*," said Hilly grimly.

Rebecca was already unstrapping a twin, who attached herself sleepily to her grandmother without waking, like a small soft octopus. Hilly, trying to use the same technique, found herself attacked by a fractious, suddenly woken, and very angry Ben, who screamed at the top of her voice that she was being stolen by a very wicked mummy.

"You're so much better with them than I am," Hilly said tiredly to Rebecca.

Somehow the twins and the bags and the hastily bought flowers and chocolates were unloaded, and soon they were all recovering in Rebecca's wonderfully ramshackle farmhouse kitchen, where wooden spoons and kitchen knives rubbed up alongside paintbrushes in jars, and painting canvasses were stacked up against the Aga to dry out.

Rebecca put a huge drink in front of Hilly, and put the twins at either end of a massive sofa, with a blanket over them.

"One of two things will happen," she said comfortingly. They'll go back to sleep, or they'll make a den. Now. Fill me in on all the news. Have you heard from Atticus?"

"He sent an email yesterday, and a text, just before we got here. He seems fine. More than fine."

"Is he having a lovely time? What did his friend want?"

"I'm not sure. He still wasn't sure. Maybe it was just a catch up, you know a conscience thing."

"Men don't really do that, do they? But anyway, it's nice he got in touch with Atticus. After so many years. Especially after, well you know, all the trouble."

"After Flora."

"Yes. Well. Did Shorty, what's his name?"

"Salty."

"Salty. Right. Did he know Flora, or about what happened?"

"I don't know, I suspect not."

"Probably for the best. Atticus needs to have friends. And I'm sure he'll be a help, if help is required."

"And meanwhile, he gets to stay on a yacht in the sun, whilst *I*,..."

"Don't be bitter Darling, it doesn't suit you. It's just because you're tired."

"Do you think?" Hilly was seriously considering putting her head onto her arms and dropping off right there on the kitchen table.

"And although it is sunny, The Canary Islands isn't quite the paradise you're imagining."

"Really? It always looks pretty good to me. He sent me a picture. I think he was at some sort of party.

There was a very glamorous piece on the deck of a yacht with a glass of champagne in her hand. What's not to like?"

"Well everywhere has its dark side."

Rebecca was wandering about the kitchen opening and closing cupboard doors. Hilly knew that although she seemed to be pottering about aimlessly, very soon there would be a wonderful supper on the table. Rebecca was a dab hand with a *le creuset* cooking pot and a *daube of beef*, without ever seeming to chop an onion.

"Ma. It's a *holiday*. On a *boat*. With an old *friend*."

"Venice was a *holiday*. With an old *friend*. In a posh hotel, and look what happened then!"

"Well that was different. Laura Hutchinson was hardly a friend."

"As it turned out. That poor girl."

"Salty's lovely. I remember him. He and I....."

"Was he one of yours?"

"Well it was a long time ago."

"You were so pretty then. Anyway, I've been looking at Tenerife. On the internet."

"Ma! You and the internet. You always seem to find things nobody else does."

"Put it this way, there are quite a few dark corners in that particular paradise. I just hope Atticus doesn't get find himself backed into any of them."

"He won't Ma. He's just on a holiday."

"Your brother isn't 'just' anything. He's like your father. He was always getting himself into scrapes too."

The *daube of beef* appeared, along with a beautiful salad full of herbs, a loaf of homemade crusty bread and an excellent bottle of red, courtesy, as Rebecca put it, of a 'perfectly sweet' old neighbour who just happened to have a wine importing business. The twins, miraculously, opted for sleep over adventure. Outside the wind got up and rain lashed the windows.

Chapter Seventeen

"Well I didn't see anything And I was here all night." Francis, gruffer than ever in his ubiquitous fishing jersey and a battered hat puffed away on a pipe as Salty paced up and down.

Neither Salty nor Atticus had slept well and Salty had been up and about well before the light had filled the harbour. He had bounded across to Francis's boat as soon as he saw the old man's head appear through his deck hatch.

"There was somebody on board," Salty protested. "Around midnight."

"Ah," said Francis. "*I will always love you.*"

"Right!" said Salty, realising a moment too late what Francis meant. "But by the time we came round, there was nobody here."

"Where were you then?" said Francis, "With that crowd of idiots in Lenny's Darts Bar?"

"Of course not. We were having dinner on *Grace Kelly.*"

"Ah, the fragrant Pookie. Well if you don't mind my saying, an evening with that girl might well cause you to start seeing things. Stars mainly."

"That had nothing to do with it. We *saw* someone. On *Cangreco*. Moving about. And by the time we got back, it was too late!"

"Anything missing?"

Salty sighed. "No. But there were signs of disturbance."

"Disturbance."

"Yes! Things moved. Someone has been through my files. And Atticus's cabin is a mess."

"Perhaps Atticus isn't a very tidy person."

"Right." Salty gave up. "Well thanks anyway."

Francis continued puffing away but said no more.

"Look, we really should talk to the police," Atticus, said half an hour later, still trying to placate Salty. It wasn't easy to pace thirty six feet of boat with such long legs, but Salty was managing it.

"They'll be useless. I've already told them about Louise but they aren't interested."

"I don't mean about Louise. I mean about the break-in."

"It wasn't exactly a break-in was it? The boat isn't locked. It rarely is when it's here. Everyone knows everyone else."

"You think it was someone you know?"

"No. Yes. Maybe. I can't believe anyone I know would do it. But then anyone else would have aroused suspicion. Strangers stand out a mile here."

"Unless they're customers. For the boat trips and things."

"Customers don't come round here at night. Sometimes when they've had a few too many in McSweeneys or Lenny's they'll fancy themselves as sailors and try and get onto one of the nearest boats, but never all the way over here."

"We should report it anyway. I'll go if you don't want to. Maybe they'll listen to a second voice."

Salty considered this. It might be worth a try. I'd just get angry with them and that definitely doesn't help. You can take the car. I'll show you where the *Guardia Civil* is. The police station."

And so it was that just an hour or so later, Atticus found himself at the wheel of the terrible Renault, puttering along the motorway in fear of his life. The champagne of the night before was still drying him out, and he was in desperate need of a long cold drink. The constant battering the car was receiving from the hard shoulder which seemed to be made up entirely of loose chippings, made his head ache. He gritted his teeth and told himself it was all in the interests of maintaining law and order. The police really did need to know about the break-in on *Cangreco,* and maybe he'd ask about Louise while he was there.

The *Guardia Civil* office was down a side street in an unpromising bit of Los Cristianos. Not for today the bright blue harbour with its busy fishing fleets, island ferries and rows of shops and cafes. The street was dark, with metal grilles locked down in front of most of the doorways and nobody but a stray dog to keep Atticus company. The police station was the only unlocked door, and going in, Atticus found himself in a dreary waiting room, lit from overhead by a fluorescent strip light, and furnished with a row of plastic chairs which had seen better days. There was nobody about.

A very old woman came in behind him and sat on one of the chairs. She looked Atticus up and down and offered him a crumpled paper bag, which he realised had an open bottle of some spirit in it. He shook his head and she snorted, offended, before taking a long drink herself and settling down.

After about half an hour, during which Atticus had knocked on the only other door in the room several times, a uniformed officer came out. He shouted a string of angry expletives at the woman who took no notice, before ushering Atticus through the door and into another room, not dissimilar to the first, but with a table in it.

"*Hablo Inglese*?" said Atticus politely.

"*Si, claro,*" said the officer in a weary voice, as he opened a file to reveal a clean sheet of paper. "Is part of job."

Taking out a pen he began to write. He carried on writing. As he got halfway down the page Atticus wondered if it was an essay, or a shopping list, or a letter to his ageing mother in Madrid. Eventually, as if noticing that Atticus hadn't gone away, he stopped and looked up.

"Si?" he said.

"I want to report a break-in," said Atticus.

"A break in?"

"Yes."

"Your hotel?"

"No. A boat."

"You have boat?"

"No. Not *my* boat, someone else's boat."

"You broke somebody's boat? Why?"

"No I didn't but someone else did."

"Why is owner of boat not here? *He* tell me of break-in."

"He's asked *me* to tell you."

"Where is boat?"

"Down at the port. It was last night, the break-in."

"The port. You are on holiday yes?"

"Yes. No. Well that's not important is it?"

"Si senor it is *very* important. You are a tourist yes? You should be on the beach. Or in the cafe. Or swimming in the pool of your hotel. And yet you are here."

"Well quite. I'm not much more enthusiastic about being here than you are. But I need you to know that somebody broke into a boat last night, and a woman has gone missing and I think the two may be connected and even if they aren't you need to make a note in that file of yours."

"File?"

"That file." Atticus indicated the paper the policeman had been writing on.

"This? Is not file. This is application."

"Application?"

"Yes. I am applying for a better job. I have to make application."

"Now?"

"Now? Yes. Why not?"

"Because *I* am here to report a crime!"

"A crime? Why didn't you say so?"

"I did."

"No, you said somebody got onto a boat. This is not crime. Is anybody dead?"

"Well no. At least I hope not."

"There you are. Go back to your holiday senor. Have a - what do you say *fab* time."

"Look here, is there anyone else I could talk to?"

"Why you want to talk to someone else? You have no friends? You have no holiday companions?"

"I have friends. A friend. Look I need to report this break-in, because I am convinced it is important.

And I want to check if you have made any progress with the disappearance of the woman."

"What woman?"

"The woman I mentioned earlier."

"You did not mention a woman."

"Yes I did. Look can you just check and see if you have filed a report of a missing woman. Her name is Louise Renton."

"Women go missing all the time. Then they come back. It is called *boyfriend* trouble" The policeman sniggered. "Or maybe they go home to where they come from. Forget that England is horrible."

"England is not horrible."

The policeman looked at him

"Well, alright. It can be. A bit. Anyway, we're getting off the point, Louise Renton is not at home in England. Her home is here. Nor is she off with some boyfriend. And what I want to know is, do you know about it?"

"I do not know about it and therefore there is no missing woman."

Atticus took a deep breath.

"Can I have a piece of that?" He indicated the writing pad. The policeman looked surprised and handed it over. Atticus leant over and took the pen out of the policeman's hand. He wrote on the paper.

Missing person. English woman, living in Tenerife. Louise Renton. Brown hair. About 155 cm. Works Paradise Properties, in Los Cristianos, on that bit where the Irish bar is, where the row of palm trees has every third one missing, and there's a tattoo shop and an ice cream place. Missing since, - Atticus was trying to remember everything Salty had said - *last Thursday. Contact* - and here he put his own name and mobile phone number, and '*care of Jose's 'Majestic Cafe' Puerto Colon.*

Then he drew a line, and under it, added   *Also: break-in on boat the Cangreco Loco, Puerto Colon.*

Then he wrote: *I hope you get a better job. At least I hope you get a job you are better at. Good luck. Hasta Luego.*

Then he gave the bemused policeman his pen back, put the page into the folder in front of him and left. As he went out, the old woman emitted a long, low and loud noise which might have been a snore, but was probably something else entirely.

He headed down the dark little street and back out into the sunshine with considerable relief and found the bar with the red seats where he and Salty had been the day before. He ordered coffee and toast and marmalade, because he forgot he was in Tenerife, and then a pint of lager when he remembered. The long cold beer helped considerably with his champagne hangover and the toast was curiously comforting. He felt his nerves settling again, as the sun warmed his face. Surely nothing *really* bad could happen here.

Chapter Eighteen

Atticus was just finishing his breakfast, when he saw the man with the long legs and the expensive deck shoes again. He was striding along the side of the harbour, his head carefully shielded by another newspaper. Atticus couldn't be sure it was him, but then again... Atticus paid for his food and got up. By the time he got to the street corner, he could just see the deckshoes turning off towards the car park. Atticus followed.

"Oi Gorgeous!" he heard a voice behind him, and turned, reluctant to let the deckshoes out of his sight. One of the girls from the tour company was running towards him. "Hi!": she said brightly. You're Salty's friend right? I'm Sooze, remember? What brings you here?"

Atticus hesitated. "He didn't want to stop but he also didn't want to seem unfriendly. "I'm just looking around," he said, "you know a few errands, bit of breakfast."

"Drinking off your party hangover more like," said Sooze, indicating the table he had just left with its empty lager glass. "Want to buy a girl a coffee while you're here? I'm off duty for another hour and then I have to go and collect the Whites from their hotel. White, funny eh, what with their middle kid being so dark. Bet he gets bullied at school. I didn't notice it when they arrived at the airport, but it's as clear as day now, he's adopted. Mixed race parentage. Poor little mite. Imagine being adopted by them."

"I'm afraid I can't stay," said Atticus not wanting to be drawn on the subject of the unfortunate Roger

White. "Things to do." Sooze looked disappointed. "Alright then," she said. "Maybe later? I'll be at the port. Amy, she's the sexier one of us..." here Sooze waited for Atticus to disagree, "She's got a bit of a problem with her rugby team, they want to go on the jeep safari, but our usual jeep guys aren't too keen. Oh well, all in a day's work!" Sooze flicked her hair and brandished her clipboard. "Have a lovely day!"

Atticus ran down to the car park. As he got there, he saw a blue pickup truck at the exit over the far side, heading uphill, in a cloud of dust.

There was no way he could catch up with the truck. In fact he couldn't even be sure he wanted to. How did he know the deckshoe man was driving the truck? Atticus leapt into the Renault and screeched out of the car park, only to discover that screeching was the most the Renault could do, and that travelling at more than thirty five was definitely not part of its repertoire. He chugged up the hill and out of town to the crossroads, where the motorway met the coast road. Opposite there was a smaller road, leading directly away from him and uphill. Atticus thought he could see a faint dust trail and with little thought to the possible danger of driving a small and unreliable car across six lanes of a motorway, pulled out. There were squealing brakes, there was hooting, there was a lot of swearing and he had made it across to the other side.

"Well done old thing," said Atticus to the Renault, mainly to discover if he was still capable of speech, and he began the climb.

When he had borrowed the car, from Salty earlier that morning, they hadn't had a conversation about petrol. Salty had probably imagined that Atticus would drive the five or so miles to the police station and another five or so back. He hadn't thought for one minute that his friend would embark on an uphill, fuel-burning chase into the mountains. If he *had* imagined it, he might have said,'you'll need to put a bit of petrol in it I'm afraid'. Or 'here's ten Euros for the petrol station, which is on the left as you go into/out of Cristianos'. Or even 'be careful, if you miss the petrol station you'll have a heck of a job finding another one within reach'.

Atticus sat on the side of the road for an hour or so. Beside him the Renault slept, empty and exhausted. Every few minutes, a lone lorry would trundle past, spilling cabbages, or oranges, or bales of hay, or even on one occasion, a surprised-looking chicken which ran off into the sparse undergrowth. He had his phone, but he had no idea who to call. Salty wasn't answering, and Atticus could picture him on *Cangreco*, hosing down the deck or fixing a winch, the stereo playing U2 at full volume, while the phone buzzed unnoticed on the galley table. Atticus had left a message, but with little hope of an imminent rescue.

Suddenly there was a screech of brakes, and a tiny yellow sports car skidded to a stop within an inch of his bumper. A cloud of dust obscured his vision and he was glad his sunglasses had stopped a good amount of it going straight in his eyes.

"Good Heavens Atticus, whatever are you doing up here?"

It was Pookie, in full Audrey Hepburn mode, a silk scarf protecting her platinum hair from the dust, huge dark glasses obscuring her face, and wearing a pair of very sexy white jeans, a scarlet linen shirt and impossibly high-heeled sandals.

Chapter Nineteen

"I've never been so glad to see anyone in my life," Atticus said, accepting a madly social kiss. "I was just going, well for a drive really. I should have asked about petrol." He looked ruefully at the Renault.

"Oh God Salty's so mean about petrol!" said Pookie, "He's always lending that car to people, just as it runs out. It's his way of making sure he never has to put any in it. The nearest petrol station is down on the motorway. Look, I'll drive you down, we'll pick up a can and come back later. Hop in!"

Obviously Atticus's journey back down to the main road was much more glamorous than his journey up had been, but he was still anxious. The more he thought about it, the more sure he was that he *had* been following deckshoe man, and also that deckshoe man had in some way, been following *him*.

Pookie drove at extreme speed along the motorway, ignoring the very different type of hooting and whistling she was attracting, before pulling suddenly in to a petrol station. Leaping out of the car, she swung her handbag over her shoulder.

"Come on," she said, "we'll have a drink first."

Life really was very different here, reflected Atticus as they found seats along a stainless steel bar which looked down over the petrol pumps. A couple of boiler-suited youths had already begun polishing Pookie's car, giving her the thumbs-up first, before she waved enthusiastically back.

"Lovely boys," she said, "D'you know, they can't do enough to help?"

She ordered a bottle of rose wine which appeared in a very nice steel ice bucket, complete with good glasses and a plate of olives.

"Don't tell anyone," she said. "Officially I only drink champagne, but needs must. This is a petrol station after all."

Atticus pictured the service stations he knew back in England, with their fast food outlets and dreary displays of soft toys, inflatable neck cushions and sweets.

The olives were wonderful, plump and briny, and were swiftly followed by tiny plates of octopus salad and the local *patatas bravas,* impossibly small wrinkled potatoes in a fiery tomato sauce. The wine was cold and crisp and as he sat there next to the extraordinary Pookie, her sports car glinting in the sunshine ready for their return trip, and the wine chasing away the last vestiges of last night's party, he felt like a million dollars.

"So," said Pookie, "what *exactly* were you doing on the road to *Parque del Teide*? And *don't* tell me you were sightseeing, because there's precious little up there until you get to the top and then it's a bloody volcano. Not even an active one."

Atticus thought for a moment. Should he confide in Pookie? He had fallen for the wiles of a beautiful woman before and had got very severely burned. Only a few months ago, he had really believed that the beautiful socialite Laura Hutchinson had remembered him from school, and that she'd been pining for him ever since leaving the Sixth Form. She had bought him lunch at the Dorchester and given him tickets to a party in Venice. And just as he had begun to live the dream, he had discovered it was a nightmare, and he was just a pawn in a very unpleasant game. No, he wasn't about to fall for that again - was he?

Pookie was looking intently at him. "Don't be silly," she said. "If I wanted you to make love to me, I'd have said so. You're lovely, but you're just not my type."

Atticus decided to take the risk. He had already realised he wasn't really equipped to handle the whole car chase thing on his own.

"I went to the *Guardia Civil* this morning," he confessed.

"Good Lord *why*? said Pookie. "They're hopeless."

"Yes," admitted Atticus. "I know that now. Anyway I told them about the break-in on *Cangreco* and that Louise was missing. And they weren't interested at all."

"No surprises there. Now you've done that, what's next?" said Pookie.

"This is going to sound very silly," said Atticus.

"Go on," said Pookie, pouring the last of the wine into his glass and signalling for another bottle. The drink-driving laws were obviously very different here too.

"Salty showed me a picture of Louise. And I think the person who took that photograph, is following me. He was sitting behind us in a cafe yesterday."

"However do you work that out?" said Pookie.

"Well it was his shoes really. Distinctive."

"Just a coincidence surely?"

"That's what I thought," said Atticus, "but then when I came out of the police station this morning, he was there. And by the time I got back to the car, he was heading up that road. So I followed him."

"How intrepid you are! And you're *sure* it was the same man? What does he look like?"

"That's the thing. I've only seen his legs."

Pookie laughed, throwing her head back, a really good laugh which rang out across the forecourt. She really could stop traffic, thought Atticus.

"You are so funny!" she said. "You think you've seen this man three times, but you only recognise him by his legs?"

"And his shoes," Atticus reminded her.

"Oh well, *now* you're talking," said Pookie. "Of course you *can* tell pretty much everything you need to know about a man by his shoes. His shoes and his wristwatch."

"Can you?" said Atticus, looking at Salty's borrowed deck shoes, and fiddling with the classic watch his Godfather Horatio had given him.

"Absolutely," said Pookie. "You see I know that you are a true gentleman because of that lovely watch, and that you have borrowed the shoes because a true gentleman would have shoes that fit properly. I also know you borrowed those shoes from Salty because they have green paint on them from when we were both helping to respray the hull of that old curmudgeon Francis's manky boat. Not that he was remotely grateful, grumpy bugger."

"I shall call you Shoe Sherlock," said Atticus.

"So what kind of shoes was your stalker wearing?" Pookie asked.

"I'm afraid they were deck shoes too," admitted Atticus, "although they were in better nick than these. More expensive too I should think. The ones with the two-tone leather sole and the tassells."

"Mmmm *Du Barry*," said Pookie, knowledgeably. "Probably. Or *Sebago*. Nice. But not exclusive I'm afraid."

"I know. Even I'm thinking this all sounds a bit tenuous," agreed Atticus. "He was driving a blue pick-up. At least if it *was* him."

They finished their lunch with more cheerful talk of boats and cars and as they got back to the car Atticus noticed two bright green petrol cans on the back seat. Pookie blew kisses to the mechanics and attendants and they roared off back the way they'd come, leaving the motorway to head up the hill road almost without slowing down.

"Hold onto your hat!" shouted Pookie above the roar of the little car's engine.

"Look," she said a few moments later, as they pulled in behind the little Renault. "Why don't we go a bit further up? See if we can see that truck. Your car'll never survive the journey, and I'm curious now. I know a few people who live up here, there are a couple of out-of-the-way villas. Maybe your deck shoe man is one of the residents. Maybe he's someone I know, and we can introduce you, make friends, put your mind at rest?"

For some reason Atticus suddenly felt very sure he was not going to want to make friends with deck shoe man, but he told himself not to be so silly. Pookie unloaded the petrol cans into the boot of the Renault, fired up the little car, and they roared off again.

A few hundred yards up the road, they passed the entrance to what looked like a substantial building site. "New apartments!" shouted Pookie."Smartest on the island they say. Timeshare. I went to a party in their sales suite. *Very* spesh. Even *I* was tempted. And I already own several things here."

Atticus looked down the driveway to where a white Moorish-style palace was halfway constructed. Rolling green lawns stretched away from it towards the sea.

"Very expensive I expect," he shouted back.

"You'd be surprised," said Pookie. "They have ways of making it affordable. But you be careful. Not all of their ways are customer-focused." She gave him an odd look over the top of her sunglasses, before turning her eyes back to the winding road.

Chapter Twenty

As they climbed into the hills, the air above the open-top car grew noticeably thinner, and by the time they had passed through about half a mile of pine trees, Atticus felt as though they were reaching the top of the world. The wine and the company made him light-headed, and he wanted nothing more than for Pookie to pull over and spread a rug onto the floor of the forest so they could have a little sleep. But that was before he saw the blue pickup truck.

"Pull over!" he shouted, and as Pookie executed a near-emergency stop, he pointed.

"That's it," he said, "That's the truck I saw leaving the harbour. That's Deckshoe man's truck."

Pookie pulled off the road and they walked over to where the truck was parked under the last of the trees, by a wide iron gate weighed down by a substantial padlock.

"Very welcoming," said Atticus, looking at the padlock.

Pookie was walking round the truck. "It looks like a very ordinary pick up to me," she said. "I don't think I've seen it before. But this place I *do* know."

"You know it?" said Atticus.

"Yes," said Pookie. "But I've never been in. It belongs to someone big."

"Big as in tall?" said Atticus already knowing the answer.

"Big as in large involvement. Big as in *Mr* Big. Big as in..."

Pookie's voice tailed off.

"What?" said Atticus.

"Big as in you don't want to know," said Pookie. Her eyes were focused on the drive. Atticus looked.

Coming out of the trees towards them, was a thickset man with some very impressive muscles bulging under a black T-shirt and tracksuit trousers, talking into a two-way radio. There was a leather strap round his shoulders that he had only seen people wearing in films. The kind of films where thick-set men in black T-shirts carried guns.

"What do we do now?" whispered Atticus

"I'm working on it" answered Pookie.

"Could you work on it a bit quicker?"

"Follow my lead."

The man reached the gate and leant on it.

"Hi!" said Pookie brightly. The man didn't answer.

"Ola!" Pookie tried again. "*Habla Espanol*?"

"Is that it?" whispered Atticus.

"I'm a friend of, um..." Pookie waved a pretty hand in the air, as if the name she was trying to remember was only just beyond her. "The thing is, we were just having a lovely drive up in the forest, and we were passing and I just wondered if ..um..if *he* was in, so we could pop in and say Hi and have a bit of a catch up?"

The man on the gate still didn't speak.

"I mean we're not *best* friends of course, or you'd know me! And I'd know you of course. But we are pretty close. Well we were at one point. D'you know I remember a *wonderful* party, over at Santa Barbara, on the golf course, a *fabulous* villa, although not *nearly* as fabulous as this one of course, and anyway I was there and ...um,, *he* was there, and we got on *so* well. 'You must come to my place Pookie!' he said, 'drop in any time!' and I said I would, and then, well *you* know how it is, you sort of lose touch and silly me, it went completely out of my head - until *now*! And here we are, so if we could come in, and say hello that would be *great!*"

The man didn't move.

"Unless the person you're referring to *is* called *Um*," said Atticus, "I don't think we're moving in the right direction if you don't mind me saying."

The man on the gate shifted slightly, and for a brief moment Atticus thought he might be about to open the gate, but instead he took a very heavy looking handgun out of a holster and examined it closely.

"In fact I'd go so far as to say we're moving in the *wrong* direction," Atticus added. "The wrongest of a number of possibly wrong directions."

"Oh come *on,*" said Pookie to the man. "You know ..um..*he*... wouldn't like it if he knew you were keeping some good friends away would he? Why don't you just open this little gate and we'll pop in and say hi, and we can all get reacquainted!"

The man looked Pookie very thoroughly up and down, before turning his attention to Atticus. He felt as though the heat of the afternoon was tearing his head open. "Hi," he said, as brightly as he could manage. "I've never met...um ...*him* actually, I'm just a visitor was to the island. But hey! any friend of Pookie's is a friend of mine!"

The man turned as if to leave. A big patch of sweat was clearly visible down the back of his black T-shirt, running the length of the death's head skull which was pictured on it.

"Billy!" shouted Pookie suddenly. "Billy won't be at all happy with you, when I tell him!"

Atticus looked at her. "*Really*?" he said in amazement.

The man turned back. He put the gun back in its holster and with some difficulty twisted the combination locks on the huge padlock and opened the gate.

"Lucky guess," said Pookie.

They followed the security guard down the long track, to where the thickly-planted scrub hedges thinned out and the path opened out to reveal a huge yellow mansion, with a pink, pillared entrance and high arched windows, in the style of an old baroque palace, although judging by the colour of the stone, this building was quite new. Palms had been planted in wide rows to either side, and Pookie and Atticus glimpsed lawns and fountains in the gardens beyond. Two huge SUVs with blacked-out windows were parked outside.

"Billy," said Pookie quietly. "Billy." Now, all I have to do is remember all the Billys I know and try to work out which one this is."

"*What*?" said Atticus, as they followed the security guard up the steps and into the house. The big man indicated a large wide glass bowl on a table just inside the door. The bowl was full of mobile phones. They all looked at it.

"Can we pretend we don't have one?" said Atticus quietly.

"I don't think so," said Pookie.

They each put a phone in the bowl, their discomfort giving way momentarily to wonder, as they found themselves standing under a huge and ornate glass dome. In the centre of the vast atrium was another fountain, this one a collection of bronze and stone statues, with water cascading from the mouths of cherubs and dragons. The marble floor was equally impressive, a series of mosaics in terracotta and blue and gold.

"Good heavens," said Pookie faintly.

"I love an understated interior," said Atticus.

Their lumbering companion had disappeared, and they stood around trying to take in the opulence of their surroundings.

"Do you think Billy is at home?" said Atticus, after about twenty minutes.

Chapter Twenty-One

"Listen!" said Pookie. Atticus stopped what he was doing which was a sort of soft-shoe-shuffle meets-hopscotch on the complicated pattern of the floor and listened. Faintly in the distance they could hear music.

"I can hear people," said Pookie. "Screaming."

"Screaming?"

"Or laughing. Yes, that's it. Laughing…Probably."

They crossed the floor to the far side of the hall where huge french windows looked out over the landscaped gardens. Sprinklers whizzed water across the lush grass.

"Lucky water isn't in short supply on the island," said Atticus.

"It is," said Pookie. "You're only supposed to use grey or black water for watering. And even then there are certain times of the year when you're only allowed if you're a golf club or a tourist resort. People forget that this is a volcanic island. Black sand, dry rock, red dust. All this rolling greenery and all the white sandy beaches are faked."

"Grey or black water?"

"Grey is re-used, recycled. Bathwater, rainwater, that kind of thing."

"Black?"

Don't ask.

"That looks like lovely clean water."

"It does doesn't it?"

Atticus tried the door handle and the French windows opened out onto a small terrace dotted with exotic plants in ornate coloured ceramic pots. There were little stone archways to either side and they followed the sound of the music, which got louder as they went, and was soon accompanied by splashing sounds.

"I think we're about to gatecrash a pool party," said Pookie. "Ready?"

They turned a corner to find that they were indeed, at a pool party. A series of four swimming pools all at different levels, followed the stepped landscape to where the last, an infinity pool seemed to drop off the side of a cliff. By the side of each one were rows of curtained beds, like striped tents, some complete with reclining incumbents, some with the curtains very much drawn, and some vacant. Atticus felt sorely tempted to have a little lie down. All round the pools, and scattered over the terraces were people in bright coloured clothes, the young women in tiny bikinis and barely-there swimsuits, the slightly less blessed in silk wraps. The men wore board shorts and dressing gowns, or lounged in the sun in the smallest of swimming trunks. Waiters in hot little uniforms circulated with trays of drinks. At the far end of one of the pools, a tall elegant man in dark glasses and wearing a good deal of gold jewellery had set up a series of record decks and was mixing what Atticus believed were known as 'sounds'.

"Wow," he said.

"I can't think why that man made such a fuss about letting us in," said Pookie in an offended tone. "Everyone's here. Even Madeleine Trent and her ghastly toyboy. And look! see that gnome-like bloke over there in the salmon-coloured beach shorts? That's Harry Webberly. Imports Mercedes' in Santa Cruz. Rumour has it some of them still belong to people on the mainland. Those two men in the steel grey silk suits? They run timeshare developments along the coast. They're the ones you *don't* want to be buying from. And that chap in the terrible baggy green trunks? That's Michael O Gorman. Nobody knows what he does, but he's had four wives, each younger and more beautiful than the last, and every couple of years he disappears for three months at a time, usually bringing a new one back with him. And invariably without remembering to divorce the previous one. They say he's on the run, but nobody knows exactly what he's on the run from."

Atticus stared at the scene. "Is there anybody here who isn't a criminal?" he asked.

"I doubt it," said Pookie.

"Except us." said Atticus.

"Well yes. You're obviously as honest as they day is long. The thing is, that's going to make you stand out a bit. And if there's one thing that career criminals don't like, it's an outsider."

"Surely the one thing they really don't like is the police?"

Pookie laughed sympathetically. "Oh no darling. The police are no problem here. Not for this lot. Look at that bearded chap in the Speedos. He's something terribly important in the *Policia Nacional*. That's the bit of the law that deals with serious stuff. *El honor es mi divisa,* that's their motto. Honour is my emblem."

"Irony is my watchword?" said Atticus.

"Exactly. So if we're going to fit in here, we're going to have to join in."

"What? *How*?" said Atticus, as a waiter came over with a tray of drinks. Pookie raised her sunglasses and peered at him intently. Then, taking a glass of champagne from the tray, strode confidently forward.

"*Circulate,*" she hissed at him. "Avoid telling them the truth and they'll make it up."

Confused, Atticus watched her. "Madeleine!" she shouted happily, waving, "How *are* you dear? Over that little trouble with your hormones? *Do* hope so? And how's the *delicious* Carlos? Lucky *lucky* you!"

"You in the business?" said a snuffly voice close to Atticus's elbow. He looked down to see a very short man in a pair of yellow trousers and little else looking up at him.

"Could be," said Atticus, trying to be enigmatic. "You know how it is." The man nodded approvingly.

"Times is hard," he said. "Times is hard." He shook his shaggy little head and stared into his drink.

"Right," said Atticus. In the distance Pookie had moved on to Michael O Gorman, who was clearly taking a more than professional interest in whatever she had to say.

Yellow trousers made an odd noise and looking down, Atticus realised the man was crying. "Oh God" he said. "It can't be *that* bad, surely?"

"You ask Billy," the little man said through sobs. "You just ask him. Ask him what happened to little Mr Tumnus. That's what they call me. See what *he* says. Then you come to me and say it ain't so bad."

"Right," said Atticus again, "Well I might just do that. Now, I can't seem to see Billy at the moment, have you seen him at all?"

Mr Tumnus looked up, his tears forgotten, a surprised look on his face. "You mean you can't see him? What are you a *blind* person? He's there, right in front of you!"

Atticus was looking at a huge man, his vast fleshy stomach protruding from the lapels of a full-length striped silk dressing gown. Several virtually naked women were hanging round him, stroking his arms and face, posing like racehorses on teetering heels. "Oh of course," he said. "Silly me, there he is! No glasses with me. Couldn't see the wood for the er....*trees.*"

"Man you got it bad," said Mr Tumnus. "You got it so bad you make me feel like *I* don't have it so bad."

It was just the *Sopranos* accent that was truly bad, thought Atticus, wondering how he could communicate Billy's presence to Pookie.

He began by waving in her direction, discreetly at first. Then, realising discretion wasn't going to work, made the gesture much bigger. So big in fact, that he knocked a drink clean out of the hand of the person standing next to him. In the resulting confusion, during which time the person turned out to be a very *very* old lady with a surprising repertoire of swear words available in both Spanish and English, he missed the moment when Pookie encountered Billy, and sadly she missed the necessary information Atticus had been trying to communicate.

Atticus looked up from the broken glass and the quivering headdress of the decrepit Boadicea to see Pookie being very firmly escorted by Billy towards him. Behind Billy was the security guard who, despite being at such a lovely party, hadn't apparently cheered up at all.

Chapter Twenty-Two

Just a couple of miles away, unaware of his friend's plight, Salty had finished hosing down the deck of *Cangreco*, and was sitting in the cockpit with a cold beer, scrolling through the pictures of Louise on his phone. Around the port, people were beginning early preparations for the fiesta, putting out flags and signs offering discounts and special menus. Holidaymakers were beginning to be caught up in the excitement and various street traders were doing good business in masks and wigs and *Sardina* T-shirts. Salty knew he should be enjoying it. But he wasn't.

Cupcake Tours' Amy came down the pontoon bearing a brace of ice lollies. Handing one up to Salty she climbed aboard, which was no mean feat given the pencil skirt.

"Still no sign of Louise then?" she said sympathetically. Salty shook his head.

"Where's that nice friend of yours? Didn't I see him heading off in your terrible car this morning?"

"You did. He went to Cristianos to the *Guardia.*"

"Good God *why?*"

"We think someone broke in to the boat last night, While we were on *Grace Kelly* with Pookie."

"Yeah, lucky you, that looked gorgeous. Still, we had a laugh, me and the boys. Until they all fell over and one of them fell in the harbour. The ambulance took ages, and by the time it arrived Gary had got out of the water and gone back to the bar, so we all had a few more with the ambulance drivers. A break-in though? Really?"

"Well to be honest I'm not sure now. We were pretty certain we saw someone last night. Bird said he'd go and report it. I know, I *know* there's not much point but he's from England, and it might help. They do care a bit about damaging the tourist trade. He has been a while though. I would have expected him to be back by now."

"Perhaps he stopped for lunch somewhere. Or maybe your car broke down again. Or maybe he ran out of petrol?"

Amy was teasing him. "Ah," Salty said, looking more closely at the phone. "Oh dear. There *is* a message." He opened the text. "Well that explains it anyway."

"What?" said Amy, still laughing, "You don't mean he *did* run out of petrol? You evil bastard! He could have got mown down on the hard shoulder, or got lost looking for a gas station! You'd better call him back, and see what's happened. Worst case scenario I'll get one of the tour buses to go out and rescue him."

Salty dialled Atticus's number. "The phone rang. And rang, and rang."

"I just can't seem to do anything right," he said sadly, giving up.

"Come on misery guts," said Amy. "You can do something right for me. I came to ask you a favour as it happens. The lads want to go on this jeep tour, and Mick and Mack have said no. You wouldn't have a word would you? I can't find anyone else to take them, and I can't imagine what they'll get up to if they're cooped up in their resort all day tomorrow."

Salty laughed. "Poor you. A whole rugby team too much for you?" he said, "You met your match finally?"

"Don't," said Amy, "It's what my mum always says, Be careful what you wish for. Sooze is no use because she's too caught up mooning over Jules, and Jules is no use because, well he's just no use really. I don't think he's going to last long at Cupcake, he doesn't seem to me to be really committed. Anyway, Sooze has her tour group to deal with. The White's have gone AWOL, and that posh woman is threatening to sue because one of her daughters spent the night with the fire-eater we hired to entertain them at the Canarian Feast. The young couple have barely left their room, and Sooze is worried that the boy, Rob is it? hasn't eaten anything for three days, so all in all it's shaping up to be a pretty tough week. And we haven't even got to the Fiesta yet!"

Salty finished his ice lolly. "Bribery won't get you everywhere," he said, "but I'll have a word with Mick and Mack later. Bring them over to the Sailors' Arms up at the crossroads later."

"Salty you are an *angel*," said Amy kissing him. "You know I'm sure Louise will show up soon. Who could possibly leave *you*?"

And she was gone, scurrying up the pontoon and back to where the rugby team were roaring their approval of an all-girl yacht racing crew who had arrived to spend the night in the port, prior to continuing on to the Azores.

Chapter Twenty-Three

"I think we were really in there," Pookie said, as they got back into the car. Atticus looked back to where the security guard had secured the gate with a crash behind them and was now pointing his gun at them. The blue pickup truck had gone.

"Yes, we were having such a *lovely* time, weren't we?" said Atticus, turning the phones, which had been rather sulkily returned, over in his hand. He registered a missed call from Salty. "Fine to tell me there's no petrol in the car *now,*" he said out loud.

Pookie drove them back down to where the offending vehicle still sat in the dust. She held the petrol cap while he filled the tank from the petrol cans they had collected from the *Disa* station.

"Well you can't say I don't take you to all the best places," she said.

"I certainly can't," he admitted. His spirits which had been raised by a combination of excitement, fear and being with Pookie, were beginning to sink. "Will I see you later?"

"Of course you will," said Pookie. But she didn't say when.

Atticus drove back towards the port, as the afternoon's tour buses were pulling away from the harbour after their passengers' days out on the water. He was already beginning to feel like a local, driving against the flow of the tourist traffic, becoming familiar with the best times to avoid the rush, hanging around at pool parties with international villains. He realised he hadn't made contact with home for a while, and stopped to send an email at the Sailors Arms.

The Sailors Arms was a bar popular with the working people of the port, less so with the tourists, as it offered only the most basic of Canarian food, a pork chop with garlic alioli, goat rib barbecue, the occasional octopus, all good, but with no frills at all. The Sailors' offered no karaoke or live entertainment, discouraged pub games and had no television, widescreen or otherwise. Only the locals were permitted to use the small internet-friendly office at the back, and by agreement, they kept it their secret. The bar however, was pretty enough to be romantic if required, and quiet enough to give a harassed yacht captain or his best friend, a bit of time and space to think.

As he connected his phone to the bar's wi-fi, Atticus saw a message from Pookie, with a picture attached. The picture was of him, standing right in the middle of the pool party. His first thought was that he didn't look too bad. The legs were beginning to take on some colour, and his dark blue polo shirt looked almost expensive. He didn't stand out like a sore thumb in the crowd at all. He forwarded the picture to Hilly. It would amuse her.

It was only a moment later that he remembered the glass bowl, full of confiscated mobiles.

"**You see Darling,**" Pookie had texted under the picture, "**The secret is to stay one step ahead. #twophones**"

Chapter Twenty-Four

In Devon, the rain was lashing at the windows. Along the coast the palm trees and Palm Courts of what is poetically termed the English Riviera were taking a beating, and dog walkers faced into the gales at their peril, hoping their small terriers and dachshunds wouldn't be washed into the sea. It had been dark for most of the afternoon and now the evening threatened darker skies still. It was hard to imagine the sunny days of an English Spring would not be far away, or indeed that they had ever existed.

Bill and Ben had settled thoroughly into their grandmother's huge, shabby house, and were tearing about in what Rebecca liked to call her Drawing Room, making wigwams and demanding Nutella and Twiglets. Hilly, who had been trying to set up a FaceTime call with Hal, who hated FaceTime and was, she suspected, deliberately failing to switch it on properly, saw Atticus's email arriving, and called Rebecca to come in and share it.

"He says he hopes we're having a lovely time in rural Devon," she said grimly. Rebecca, who was not best pleased at having been distracted from the beginnings of another huge canvas in her American Indian series, sighed.

"I suppose he thinks that's funny," she said, sinking into a chair, several layered, paint-pattered cardigans wrapped round her.

"He says we should be proud of him because he's partying with the natives," Hilly read on.

Rebecca sat up. "Oh dear. That sounds ominous," she said.

"Ma," protested Hilly. "He's just having a good time. He's always been able to make friends. I remember when we were young I used to take him with me to parties, because he would go up to strangers and chat to them happily for hours about U-boats, or matchboxes, or the finer points of racehorse training, until they were so bored they'd be pleased to see *me*."

"He believes the best of everybody. But remember Venice." said Rebecca.

"Well he doesn't seem to be in any trouble here. He says they're all lovable rogues. Hang on, he's attached a picture.....Look! - now that *does* look like a good party!"

Outside the storm got more intense, and the straggling honeysuckle and climbing roses which Rebecca was always meaning to cut back, whipped the sides of the house and rattled the windows. The twins screamed in a combination of fear and excitement, and Hilly was forced to break away from the screen to intervene. By the time she got back, Rebecca was sitting at the desk.

"Doesn't it make you wish for sunshine Ma?" said Hilly.

Rebecca pointed at the picture of Atticus at the party. "There are some faces I never thought I'd see again," she said, "That's Michael O Gorman. I'm sure it is. And that's Billy Flynn. Although they both look a lot older than I remember."

"You know these people? Is that good or bad? Should *I* know them?" said Hilly.

"No Darling, you should most definitely *not,*" said Rebecca.

"But you do?"

"No of course not," Rebecca shut the laptop with a snap. "No, I'm probably mistaken. It really is so dark in here!"

"We ought to send an email back to Atticus," said Hilly. "What shall I say?"

"Tell him to get on with it. He must learn to stand on his own two feet. I often think that's where I went wrong with you two. I gave you far too much attention and far too much help. Now I need to think." She got up. "And I need to prep canvas."

Hilly, left alone in the study, suddenly felt like a very small child again. As far as she could remember, Rebecca had given her the scarcest of attention or help. But then she wasn't Atticus.

She opened the laptop again. A bit of research wouldn't do any harm, she told herself. What were the names Ma had mentioned?

Suddenly, the room was lit up by a brilliant flash of white lightning. Outside, the sea raged up against the cliffs, and there was another crash from the drawing room. Then the lights went out.

"Bugger!" shouted Rebecca from then other end of the house, where her studio, a sort of haphazard orangery attached to the seaward end of the property, was situated. "Power outage! We need Gin and we need ice cream!"

"Jean Jean, Jean and Scream!" shouted Bill and Ben. "We want Jean!"

Hilly, felt her way past stone-cold radiators and a good amount of dark furniture with pointed corners, out towards the kitchen in search of candles. Atticus, on his sunny, party-filled bloody *holiday*, would have to wait.

Chapter Twenty-Five

"Look up there Barry," said Shell, pointing up the side of the hill to where she could see people standing on the edge of what looked like landscaped gardens. Behind them, she could make out the turrets of a Baroque mansion. "Look Barry! There's another resort up there, I *said* there's another one! Look, those people look very smart don't they? This is a very posh bit of the island, you know, it's quite the best bit. I *said* if we're going to live here, we might as well live in the best bit eh Barry?"

Barry and Shell White were standing on the small sun terrace of a two-bedroomed apartment, in the barely-finished bit of a decidedly *un*finished residential property development. In the apartment behind them a pin-striped suited man with a shiny face and aviator sunglasses who went by the name of Degsy was arguing loudly on his phone, ostensibly to his boss.

"I *know* mate, I *know,*" he was saying, "but as I told you, if my customers want two weeks' red time in apartment 408, they want two weeks red time in 408 and I don't care if you have to re-schedule the build to accommodate them, you just effing well do it!"

"He seems to be going to a lot of trouble for us," said Shell after a while, "Perhaps there's a bit of a problem."

"Yeah," said Barry eventually, "There is a problem. And the problem *is* that he can rebuild this whole bloody resort and we still won't be able to afford to buy a sodding timeshare!"

"Come on now Barry, we've been through all this!" said Shell. "Degsy's explained it all. The finance and all that. The way he works it out, it's cheaper than staying in a hotel every year, and you've got to admit, the apartments are beautiful. I mean what's not to like about two bathrooms, and both en-suite? You're always complaining Bex is too long in there. And remember the extras too Barry! There are going to be *four pools*, one specially for the kiddies, Tyne'll love that, and a Kids Club for those long afternoons when we just want a bit of peace and quiet..."

"Don't suppose they have a wives' club do they?" said Barry, thinking momentarily of peace and quiet.

"Oh *you*," said Shell fondly, "And there's the monorail, planned to go right down the the beach, Degsy says, and three restaurants, one authentic local, I guess that's like a Taverna, you loved that fish place in Kefalonia, didn't you Barry? And an oriental buffet, and one of those posh fine dining ones, and that's as well as the pool bars and the Alhambra Grill! Ooh, I won't be able to choose where to eat first!"

Barry looked out at the expanse of bare red earth which stretched from the terrace they were standing to the boundary of the resort. A lone and unmanned earthmover sat forlornly in a hole, wide caterpillar tracks were beginning to be filled in by the dust of weeks of inaction, and tarpaulins stretched over dwindling stacks of building materials were beginning to show signs of wear.

"Not much sign of the Alhambra Bleedin' Grill so far," he said.

"Now Barry, don't be silly. You know what Degsy said, that's all Phase Three! This is Phase One, right? That's why we have to get in now, before the price goes up! Soon as they move those builders in for Phase Two, we'll be paying twenty percent more, for the same thing, and that don't make no sense does it? I said that *don't make no sense!*"

"I've told you Shell, we can't afford it and that's that. We've been here over five hours now, and we were only going to the beach. The kids'll have caused hell in that childcare thingy, and its only fair we give them what we promised."

"Barry! Come on now, we're nearly there. Degsy says he'll make it possible even though they haven't got any apartments our size left. That's what he said. And he says all we have to do is sign up today, and then we can go. And between you and me, although I'm probably not supposed to tell you, he's promised me five tickets to the waterpark! Isn't that generous? That's customer service isn't it Barry? Customer service, thats what it's all about. Oh Barry, just think, next year, we could be sitting on the terrace of our very own apartment, looking out over our pool, sipping a cocktail, and living life like *them*." She looked up the hillside again.

Barry sighed. "I don't want to live like them Shell. I want to live like us. And that's what I can afford."

Degsy came bounding out of the apartment like a labrador let off a leash. His huge grin revealed a row of none-too-clean teeth. "Great news you two lovely people," he said, rubbing his hands together, "Great news. Call me a legend, why don't you? Call Me A Legend!"

Barry and Shell waited. "Right," said the legend, slightly deflated. "I have managed, finally, and with some considerable juggling, managed to secure you the apartment you want, 408, two weeks in red time, in perpetuity *and* for ever, for the once in a lifetime price of just twelve thousand pounds!"

Barry spluttered. Shell went as pale as it was possible for her to do considering the rapidly developing rash caused by her chosen brand of sun cream.

"Twelve thousand? You must be joking mate," Barry said. "We weren't talking about twelve. We were talking about six."

"Six? Oh no," said Degsy. "Surely not. Twelve is an extraordinary price. This is top real estate, a piece of the future, at the newest, most state-of-the-art, most expensively *specked* development in the whole of the Canary Islands. And red time, well everybody wants that don't they? Right in the middle of the school holidays. I mean, you don't want to be incurring those nasty fines the British Government is now slapping on all the poor holidaymakers who can't afford to take their kiddies to hotels at that time of year. And those people, well I feel sorry for them because they aren't going to be able to take their kiddies on holiday at all soon are they? Not with the rising cost of air fares and hotels and taxes, oh don't get me started on taxes. Now, am I right in saying, you want to be able to beat the crowd and get in at the start of this fabulous development, at the best possible price? Am I?"

"Oh yes," said Shell breathlessly, "Oh *yes*."

"And am I right, that you are a woman who appreciates the good things in life, top quality designer labels all that?"

"Oh yes," said Shell.

"And am I right in thinking you work *really* hard for the things you have, and the money you get, am I right?"

"You are!" said Shell. Barry looked at her. "At least Barry does," she conceded. "I'm a stay-at-home mum. Well it's only right isn't it? They're only kiddies once aren't they?"

"Well then. Barry, Shell, what I will say to you is this," said Degsy triumphantly. "Not only *can* you afford this, not only *should* you afford this, you *deserve* to have it. You deserve this deal, and I tell you what I am going to do, Barry and Shell. What I am going to do for you is this....

"I am going to put my job on the line."

"Um..." said Shell eventually.

"What I am going to do. Is promise you, Barry and Shell, that you can have those two weeks in red time in 408, just as you asked..."

"We didn't exactly....." said Barry. Degsy ignored him.

"And not only am I going to promise you that the apartment will be yours, in perpetuity, for those two weeks, for ever. Two weeks that you can exchange, using our patented great value global exchange programme should you, just *should* you, want to go anywhere else, although why you would I do not know...."

"Well we had wondered about Acapulco, hadn't we?" said Shell.

"*You* had," said Barry acidly. "Looks well dodgy to me."

"...and not only will I guarantee you this, but I am going to let you sign on the dotted line, here and now, with a *discount* on that amazing price I just quoted you, a discount of two thousand pounds!" Degsy finished.

"Two thousand pounds is a lot of money," said Shell, "You say you might lose your job, promising us that?"

"Two grand mate. That is a wedge" said Barry. "But then again, so is the ten grand you're still asking."

"Because I *like* you, Barry and Shell. I like you and your cute kiddies, and I want you to start having the top quality holidays you deserve right here, and *right now,*" said Degsy.

"We'd have to think about it," said Barry, "Maybe come back later in the week."

There was a long silence, at the end of which Degsy looked quite a lot less enthusiastic about Barry and Shell and their cute kiddies.

"Ah now, you see," he said through almost gritted teeth. "That isn't quite how it works."

Chapter Twenty-Six

The sun began to sink slowly, bathing the island in its customary soft pink light. A few hundred yards up from the harbour, on the terrace of the Sailors' Arms, Salty sat, nursing a long gin and tonic. He often sat there alone, watching the activity of the day slowly ease up before the night life got going. From this vantage point he could see the ferries which pottered about between the islands, the fishermen going out on the evening tide from the little fishing villages further round the coast, and in the distance, on a clear evening, he could see the island of La Gomera.

He looked at his watch. As he did so, Atticus came out of the office into the bar, having sent his email home to Devon.

"Well that was quite a day," he said, joining Salty on the terrace and ordering another gin for Salty and one for himself. "You know old man, I do think you might have mentioned the petrol situation."

"Ah, yes," said Salty, "Sorry. Hope it wasn't too much of a problem?"

Atticus remembered Pookie, and the service station lunch, the white-knuckle ride in her yellow car, the gangland pool party, and their narrow escape.

"No, no, not at all," he said.

"Good. How was the *Guardia Civil*?"

"Well you were right about them. No use at all. The one I spoke to was more interested in applying for a new job than in anything I had to say. But I filed a report anyway. Any more news this end?"

"About Louise? No."

"Or the boat? You're sure nothing is missing?"

"Doesn't seem to be. Although....."

"What?"

"Well everything was in quite a mess. So it was difficult to tell. But I'm pretty sure my books have been rifled through."

"Books?"

"My pilot books. I use them for plotting charts if we do any real sailing. I keep them in my cabin, so the punters don't drop them overboard or spill things on them. Louise loved them, She said they were beautiful, almost art." Salty's voice trailed away.

"What makes you think they've been disturbed?"

"I keep them in order, a very particular order, not alphabetical or anything anyone else would understand. And when I went to check them earlier, one was out of sequence.The one which follows the coast round past Los Cristianos as far as San Miguel, and then across to La Gomera."

"You could have moved it though?"

"I could have But I'm pretty sure I didn't. I know this coast like the back of my hand. I could have *written* the pilot book."

"And that's all that was moved?"

"I know. It doesn't sound like much does it? Nothing to distract your policeman from his CV."

There was a commotion outside, the roar of a beaten-up diesel engine and the clattering of gravel sprayed across the terrace by the wheels of a huge yellow jeep as it ground to a halt. Two chunky blonde men in red shorts and polo shirts with pictures of the same jeep embroidered on their chests leapt out, and manhandled Amy, still in her Cupcake Tours uniform after them. She untied her scarf and stuffed it in her shoulder bag, trying to make her outfit look less corporate and more like something you might wear to go out for a drink with two impossibly handsome men.

"Hell man !" shouted Mack at the bar, his Australian accent exaggerated for the audience, "What's everyone having? I need beer and I need it *now*!"

Amy came over to Salty and Atticus. "It's been a bit of a day apparently," she said "That couple, Rob, who came out with you yesterday? He and his girlfriend were on the Jeep safari today and they had a bit of a tiff and she ran off, and Mick had to go after her, which held everyone up. Rob was so embarrassed, poor guy. Anyway they made it up afterwards, and then Mack said it was even worse because they were all over each other which was a bit distracting for the other customers. And they had Imogen Brookes-Turnbull and her two daughters as well, and I think she made a pass at Mack, although to be honest that's hardly unusual. I'd make a pass at him myself if there wasn't a queue. Anyway might be an idea to wait until they've had a couple before mentioning the Rugby trip, if you see what I mean?"

Atticus laughed. "You certainly have your work cut out, don't you?" he said. "I always thought the life of a holiday rep was easy, all that sunshine and waving."

Amy looked at him. "You don't know the half of it," she said. "But if you fancy it, you know where I am. I could use a sensible down-to-earth sort like you."

Atticus wasn't sure he wanted to be seen as a sensible down-to-earth sort, but he decided to see it as a compliment.

"Anyway," Amy continued, "You couldn't be any worse than Jules. Honestly, I swear he's on another planet half the time. Turned up this morning in quite the wrong shorts."

"Good heavens," said Atticus. "Quite the wrong shorts?"

"You may think it doesn't matter," said Amy, "but if we're not instantly recognisable all the time, we can lose our punters very easily. Either because they can't find us, or because they switch to tours operated by the corporate big guys. It's about confidence in the brand."

"Oh quite," said Atticus.

Mick and Mack appeared bearing trays laden with drinks. They were obviously planning on drowning their sorrows pretty comprehensively. Atticus handed Amy a huge pink drink with an umbrella and half a rainforest in it.

"You're quite sure she isn't here?" Mack said nervously, sitting down. "Mrs B-T. You will warn me? Where is the back exit in this place anyway?"

"Don't worry mate," said Mick. "I'll let you know. As long as you're sure you don't want to go for it. She's not bad looking you know. For her age. And she's certainly keen!"

"Louise?" said Salty, who hadn't been listening.

"Not Louise," said Atticus hastily. "They're referring to Imogen Brookes-Turnbull I think she's got the hots for Mack."

"Where is Louise anyway?" said Mick, who hadn't noticed the warning looks he was getting from Amy. "She coming along later? You guys got any plans for the Fiesta?"

Chapter Twenty-Seven

Back up in the hills, darkness fell, and the limited emergency lighting shone a pinkish blue over the building site, illuminating the deserted machinery and shuttered portacabins which were dotted over the site. The only other lights in the several hundred acre site were those in the two-bedroom show apartment, where Shell and Barry were sitting side by side on the shiny chaise longue which was, as Shell muttered under her breath, not anything like as comfortable as it looked. Barry looked at his watch. They had been there for almost nine hours.

"We should be getting back," said Shell again.

"You've said that," said Barry.

"I know. But I'm worried about the kids. Where *are* they?"

Degsy, pacing up and down the length of the apartment, his cheap shoes squeaking on the tiles, sighed loudly.

"You see the thing is, I want nothing more than to let you go back to your little hotel. But I can't. I can't let you go, if you're going to turn your back on this offer. It just wouldn't be right. I might even lose my job."

"I thought you were going to lose your job if you sold it to us at that discount," Shell pointed out.

"Well, frankly Shell, there are a number of reasons why you can lose your job in this place. And I don't want to give the people who own this resort any of

TORA BARRY

them. So the thing is, the way I see it, we can all do each other a favour."

"What? Anything! I just want to go home." Barry said, exasperated.

"It's simple Barry, Simple! You sign here, give me a deposit of, let's say ten percent, credit card'll do. I'll arrange the legals, and you'll be free to go off and have a lovely dinner, secure in the knowledge you've done the right thing!"

"But I won't have done the right thing mate. With the best will in the world, I can't magic ten grand where there isn't any ten grand."

"Oh you can, Barry, you can! If I had a pound for every customer who said they couldn't afford this, and then signed up anyway, and somehow managed to afford it, well I'd have a lot of money."

"If I give you ten grand you'll have a lot of money."

"You see, you're getting there!"

"I just can't," said Barry. "I'm sorry mate, I haven't got the money and I'm not a man to spend money I haven't got. Am I Shell?"

"Apparently not," said Shell miserably.

Barry got up. "Now if you don't mind, I'd like you to let us out of here so we can collect our kids and go back to what's left of our holiday."

"We was going on that Jeep Safari weren't we?" said Shell.

"Maybe tomorrow," said Barry. "Bit late now."

Degsy continued pacing. "Ah," he said. "But that's the thing, isn't it? We never know what tomorrow will bring."

Barry looked at him. "Where I come from, that sounds like a bit of a threat," he said, "Are you threatening us?"

"You know Barry, I think, maybe I am."

Barry clenched his fists.

Shell let out a small sob. "Leave it Barry, leave it!" she said, not for the first time in their ten-year married life, "He ain't worth it!"

Barry moved towards Degsy. "We'd like to *go now*," he said, more firmly. Degsy flinched.

"Just sign it Barry," whined Shell. "It'll all work out in the end!"

"You know Barry you should listen to your wife," said Degsy in a dangerously quiet voice.

There was a long, high, ear-piercing scream. Barry looked at Shell, who looked at Degsy who had gone very pale.

"What the *hell* was that?" he said

"Roger," said Shell and Barry together.

Chapter Twenty-Eight

"No kidding mate, it's the trip of the holidays for most of the punters," Mick was saying. The Jeep Safari boys were about four pints in, and getting into their stride. "People come to Tenerife thinking it's all about lying on a sunbed by a pool all day and getting blind drunk in an Irish bar at night, but we show them what this island's really all about. The terrain is unique, this land is totally volcanic, and we can offer the real deal, right up close and personal."

"It must be quite exciting," said Atticus politely, looking at the jeep and wondering how he would fare, bounced around rocky landscape in the back of it, and whether he wouldn't, on balance, be happier with the sunbed and the pool.

"Too right," said Mick.

"But do you get people who imagine that because it's a safari, there might be wild animals to see too?"

"Hell yeah," said Mick. "And we do not disappoint, do we mate?"

"There *are* wild animals?" said Atticus. He hadn't really accounted for the possibility while he was standing by the deserted roadside halfway up the mountains a few hours earlier.

"Well not *lions* obviously," Mick conceded. "But we have a good selection of lizards. There are 6000 species of invertebrates currently on the islands. And a lot of mega-big birds."

"The real fun is the off-roading," Mack added, "We take a jeep each, and we can set up some cool drag racing, and auto-mountaineering up there."

"Not for the faint-hearted I should imagine," said Atticus.

"We tailor the trip for the clientele," said Mick. "Take today..."

"Yeah, you can keep it," said Mack into a new pint.

"That posh bird and her daughters, the daughters were well up for it, wanted to go the full assault course, but the mum, well she was easily scared. Clung to Mack like a wallaby in a sandstorm. Mind I'm not sure if she really was scared or...." Mick grinned. "Still we seem to have shaken her off."

"I wouldn't count on that," said Salty, who hadn't spoken for a while. He nodded in the direction of the road which led up from the harbour. A thin figure in a jaunty red sailing jacket was heading uphill towards them.

"Hell man," said Mack "It'd better not be......."

A few minutes later they heard Imogen Brookes-Turnbull's cut-glass accent asking for Mack at the bar. Atticus picked up Mack's drink and pointed through to the back where the office was. "Come on," he said, "we can get you out this way."

"Laters!" said Mack, who didn't need asking a second time. He picked up another full pint and followed Atticus. They heard Imogen greeting the others like long-lost relatives, with much swooping and air-kissing. "Sorry Darl," they heard Mick say with what sounded like genuine regret. "Paperwork. He got the short straw. There's a lot of it to be done in a bona fide operation like ours."

Atticus and Mack sat on a wall outside the back of the pub. The bins gave off a sour odour which sat on the night air, and the only sound was that of crickets chirruping in the undergrowth by the side of the road. Mack downed the first of his two pints.

"Ta mate," he said. "Narrow escape."

"Why don't you tell her you're not interested?" Atticus said.

"I hate hurting their feelings," Mack confessed.

"Happens a lot then?"

"Quite a bit," Mack looked sheepish. "Not always unreciprocated if you see what I mean. Can't help myself."

Atticus wondered what it would be like to be irresistible to women. Or any woman. He had hoped Pookie would be here.

"You say you were looking for Louise?" Mack said suddenly, breaking into Atticus's thoughts.

"Yes. Sort of," said Atticus. "Salty is very worried about her, and it does seem odd that nobody's seen her."

"This is a strange place," Mack said. "It looks laid back and happy but most people who come here to make a living do so for a reason, and most of us don't really talk about what that reason is."

"I'm beginning to find that out," said Atticus. "Do you think Louise might not have been entirely honest with Salty?"

"She seemed pretty straight to me," said Mack, "But all I'm saying is, you never know. When did you say she went AWOL?"

"Hard to say," said Atticus. But it seems to have been before the weekend."

"It's just that we did see her car. That little red thing she drives? I thought it was odd at the time, because it was way up in the hills. But then again, some of the smartest gaffs are up there. She was probably showing somebody a mansion. We were off roading, crashing about up there for a while, and it was still there when we drove back down again, and that was a good three hours later."

"Could you explain to me *exactly* where that was?" Atticus said.

He returned to the terrace a few minutes later. There was a faint light disappearing down the road as Mack made his way with the help of a torch down to the harbour and a bar free from predatory women, at least for a short time. Nobody else noticed. Imogen was getting over her disappointment with the help of several large vodka tonics and a local restaurant owner who bore more than a passing resemblance to Antonio Banderas and had popped in to see if the Sailors' Arms had any salad to spare. Salad, it seemed was something of a scarce commodity in a community where meat was plentiful, and quite a lot of it was goat.

"You're in luck," said Salty, as Atticus rejoined the group. Looking up, he saw Pookie, resplendent in a spangled full-length evening dress which was more than ambitious given the surroundings. "Hi Babe," she said, kissing Atticus as if they had been married for years and she had just come downstairs to join their glamorous dinner party.

"Pookie," he murmured, "You look so lovely."

"Steady on," said Mick, breaking off from an in-depth conversation with Amy about appropriate cashback arrangements for booked jeep safaris, "I'm sensing what we in Oz call an OYL situation."

"OYL?" said Atticus.

"Out of Your League," said Mick, who was at least six pints into the evening.

"Sorry," said Amy to the group, "He's had a bit of a day."

"As it happens, so have we!" said Atticus, rather looking forward to relating the tale of the day he had shared with Pookie. "Haven't we? You won't *believe* where we ended up!"

"Tell all," said Salty, "I thought you had an uneventful time in Los Cristianos?"

"That's what *you* think," said Atticus delighted. "Tell them about the pool party Pookie!"

Pookie accepted a dry martini from the barman who had mixed and brought it seemingly without being asked. She sat down, the little silk train of her dress pooling like mercury round the feet of the nasty plastic garden chair.

"Party?" she said, "That's very sweet of you. But I wouldn't quite describe our lunch at the *Disa* station as a party!"

"No," said Atticus, confused, "I meant after that. You know, up at Billy's villa?"

Pookie took a sip of her martini.

"Divine," she pronounced. "I think you caught the sun darling!" She turned to the others, "I had to rescue the dear thing from the side of the road. Salty you are very naughty. Leaving your friend with that dreadful car of yours, and no petrol!"

Atticus looked at her, a vision in apricot silk, her hair piled up on her head, a pair of very neat little amber stones in her tiny ears. OYL, he thought. OYL.

Chapter Twenty-Nine

The thing about being on holiday, Atticus reflected, as he emerged from his cabin after rather too few hours sleep, was that you could party all night and lie around all day. The thing about work is that you have to do it all day, so limiting the amount of time you can effectively party. The problem with everyday life on a holiday island was that there was no real way to distinguish which position you were in.

The port was quiet, with the only noise being that of the hoses wielded by the early birds, readying their boats for the day's excitement, and the faint clanging of the *bombona* men, dropping their barrels outside the doors of the bars along the coast. Salty was presumably still in his cabin, and Mack was still snoring contentedly on deck, having decided it was the safest option after a night out in Lenny's Darts bar rather than risking going back to his apartment, the address of which he feared he had inadvertently given to Imogen Brookes-Turnbull.

Atticus put on shorts and a new T-shirt, courtesy of Amy's promotional merchandise supply, which read '*I'm going around with the Cupcake Cuties*', hoping his deepening tan would single him out as a local in search of clean laundry rather than a holidaymaker who wanted to impress the others on his package tour.

Around the harbour, bar owners were half-heartedly wiping down chairs and tables, and starting up their industrial coffee machines. Further along the coast, Sooze and Amy were preparing for the Jeep safari, which Salty had finally managed to persuade Mick to take on, and the boys from the rugby team were still sound asleep in various apartment and hotel beds. In less than an hour they would all spring into life, like aliens awakened by a high pitched electronic signal, throw themselves into showers and appear, ready for the day's roistering at the appointed meeting place, pretty much on time. Jules, finally discovered by Sooze in the foyer of the *Hotel Araminta Princess*, with a book about the Vietnam War, had been given a list of undesirable tasks and a warning that if he didn't show a bit more willing, he would be sent straight back to the UK and a job in Customer Response Management, somewhere in Worksop.

Atticus made himself a cup of coffee in the galley and went out on deck, but unable to hear himself think above Mack's snoring, took the coffee out onto the quayside, finding a convenient spot along the harbour wall. The sun was already high, and the stone of the wall was warm. He pulled out the map which Mack had drawn the evening before on a pub napkin. It wasn't easy to read, but even to a visitor unfamiliar with the island's few roads, it was clear that the place Mack had seen Louise's car was not a million miles away from Pool Party Mansion.

Finishing the coffee and just as the first of the holidaymakers began to trickle into the port, Atticus scribbled a note to Salty, took the keys to the Renault, and left.

As he walked to the car park he rang Pookie's number. Her voicemail informed him that although Pookie was *very* grateful for his call, and although she would *love* to talk to him *very* soon, he should be aware that she was never available before 12 noon.

He headed to the *Disa* station for petrol. After all, he didn't know how long he was going to be this time.

It didn't take long to find the gate to Billy's mansion, not least because the blue pickup was back, parked at an angle by the padlocked gate. Atticus drove a little way up, and stopped behind a scrappy bush, so that the Renault was all but obscured from the road. Then he walked back down the hill and looking quickly to right and left, climbed over the gate. There was no obvious sign of any CCTV cameras, but just in case, he pretended to be consulting a tourist map which he had found in the glove compartment of Salty's car. He tried to remember any of the names he had heard yesterday, Billy, Mr Tumnus, Madeleine Trent.......

The house was quiet, and at first there was no sign that anyone was in, but as he stood carefully out of sight of the front door, he saw that the two SUVs with blacked out windows had been moved, so that they were facing outwards, their tailgates open. After a few minutes two men in black T-shirts like the one the security guard had worn yesterday appeared, carrying large wooden crates between them. They loaded them into the cars, before disappearing back inside.

He waited. Suddenly there was a rustling of the lush green rhododendron bush beside him and he jumped, turning to see the small man known as Mr Tumnus standing beside him.

"Hello again," said Atticus, trying to sound casual. "Great party yesterday eh?"

Mr Tumnus seemed to be struggling to remember Atticus. "You were there?" he said, although it seemed like a question rather than a statement.

"We talked about... business," Atticus said, "about it being a bit heavy going at the moment?"

Mr Tumnus looked unconvinced. "You involved in this?" he said, indicating the two heavy black T-shirts who had returned with another crate.

"Oh, you know," said Atticus. "Just checking the, erm..surroundings."

"I'm outa here," said Mr Tumnus. "This is too big for me. If Billy asks, say I was never here. You don't know me. I gotta go. There's a flight. If I can get to the airport I might just make it before they work out I've gone."

"Good luck," said Atticus, aware that it wouldn't be much help.

"Try the poolhouse," said Mr Tumnus suddenly. "You can't see into it from the house. Useful to know."

"What....?" Atticus was about to ask why he needed to know about the visibility aspect of the poolhouse, but the little man had gone.

He waited until the loaders had gone back inside the house and crossed the drive, so he could get round the side of the building without being seen. The gardens were quiet, the *thwack, thwack* of the sprinklers the only real noise. The terraces were clean and shining wet, and the garden furniture had been overturned, as if to prevent damage while the occupants of the house were away. Atticus stepped into the garden, and was momentarily distracted by the view. Over the layers of manicured lawns, and over the edge, down and down to where the island fell away, the sea stretched, sparkling in the sun, for miles and miles and eventually to Africa.

He was startled by a sound behind him, and darting into a nearby flowerbed, found himself only able to see the lower half of a man in shorts and deck shoes come out onto the terrace. He heard the dull chink of a cigarette lighter, felt the initial drag of man on fag. Atticus's own legs were being scratched to hell by the spiky plants in the bed, and the scratches began to itch almost immediately. Trying desperately to keep still, he realised he recognised the legs he was looking at, and those shoes.

The deckshoes paced up and down, and Atticus knew he was stuck, at least until the cigarette was finished. From where he was standing, he could see the door of the poolhouse, but his way across the lawn would be clearly within sight of the house. He stretched upward to see if he could see the rest of the smoker, but succeeded only in scratching his legs still further. Stifling a swear word, he tried to stay still, and was rewarded when the smoker, throwing the fag end into a planter on the terrace, turned and went back inside. Seizing his chance, Atticus stepped out of the flowerbed, and ran across the lawn. He dived into the poolhouse and threw himself onto one of its striped canvas bench seats, so he would be below the line of the windows.

That was when he noticed the body.

Chapter Thirty

Familiar, and yet somehow a stranger, it was odd how some*one* you knew became some*thing* you vaguely recognised once they were dead. This was, he was pretty sure, the body of something which had once been Harry Webberly, the Mercedes importer Pookie had pointed out at the party. He was dressed in a long raincoat, the front of which was open, revealing salmon-coloured beach shorts, and a garish Hawaiian beach shirt, which was torn to show a black bullet hole in the middle of a concave chest. Blood had dried round the hole, and was spreading out underneath the body, seeping into the coat's familiar checked lining, and through into a jauntily-striped rug. The gnomic face was grey, the whiskery eyebrows framing a pair of staring greeny-yellow eyes. Harry Webberly was oddly, slightly more attractive dead than he had been alive.

Atticus had seen death before. In fact, this was the second dream holiday he had been on within a year during which he had found himself lying next to a corpse. The last one had been in Venice, when he had woken up on the floor of an empty warehouse in the company of....well that was a long time ago now.

Would somebody really be murdered because they were importing stolen luxury saloon cars? Quite possibly. But why now?According to Pookie, the late Mr Webberly had been supplying luxury cars of questionable provenance to the wealthy motorists of the Canary Islands for a number of years. And why here?

Atticus lay next to the dead Webberly for a few minutes, listening for any noise outside. There wasn't any. The trouble with deck shoes is that they make no sound on flagstones. He had no idea if the deck shoe wearer was still about. Very slowly, Atticus sat up. Keeping his head very low, he peered above the sill of the poolhouse window, just in time to see the retreating back of the smoker once more, as he returned to the terrace, retrieved the still-smoking cigarette butt, took a last drag, and threw it back into the planter, before going into the house again, closing the french windows behind him.

Atticus crawled on his hands and knees to the door of the poolhouse. "I'm off," he said to the corpse of Harry Webberly.

Opening the door carefully, he continued on hands and knees out onto the lawn, keeping his options open so he could retreat if necessary. He progressed across the lawn, still without standing up, sticking tightly to the edge of the flowerbeds, until he was within reach of the French windows. Inside, nothing was moving. Atticus stood up, and keeping flat against the house, he edged towards the glass doors, eventually reaching out and trying the handle.

The door opened easily, and Atticus held his breath, but nobody came rushing to find out who was trying to get in. He peered inside. The room was dark, and there didn't seem to be anyone around. Taking his courage in both hands, he went in.

The room was cold, and not just because he'd come in out of the sun. There was no furniture, the tables and ornaments he'd noticed the day before had gone, and in their place were more of the large crates he had seen the men loading into the cars earlier. Each one would have taken at least two men to move it and there were, at first glance, about twenty of them. Atticus ran his hand along the top of one of them, feeling for a catch or a lock, but finding only rows of heavy screws where the boxes had been nailed shut. Whatever was in them?

As his eyes accustomed to the light, he saw that the boxes were unmarked, there were no labels or chalk marks, no logos or signage to tell him what was inside, where it might have come from, or who it belonged to. He was so engrossed in studying each one, that he didn't realise he was no longer alone.

And then he saw that the last box, the one nearest the door which led out into the hall and towards the front door, wasn't nailed shut. The top of the crate was just lying, at a slight angle, on the top. Atticus lifted the lid.

At first he wasn't sure what he was seeing. Dark polished wood, black metal, threatening shapes, stacked layer on layer, end to end. And then a shiver ran down his spine. Because what he was seeing was guns.

Atticus wasn't an expert on guns. In fact other than the type used by his wealthier friends and relatives on shooting weekends in the Highlands during the season, he hadn't ever seen one in real life. Now he was looking at hundreds of them. Rifles, he decided. Big, heavy-duty serious non-sporting, and definitely *unsporting*, rifles.

He reached into his back pocket and took out his phone. He had a feeling he was going to need some evidence of this. However it was unfortunate that at that very moment, Hilly chose to send him a hilarious text picture of the twins, with buckets on their heads, standing in Rebecca's garden, in front of the wreckage of a garden shed which had not survived the storm. The text played its little electronic tune. Atticus laughed at the picture, and what he saw next was stars.

Chapter Thirty-One

"Hospitals here are a good sight better than they are at home, aren't they?" said Shell, as they emerged, blinking, into the sun. "Them doctors, they really know their stuff, and they were so nice, even the foreign ones."

"They're not foreign," Barry pointed out. "It's us that's foreign here."

"Whatever," said Shell, "Anyway they patched our Roger up, and that's all that matters, isn't it Rog?"

Roger, a substantial amount of bandage and tape round his head, a foam neck collar and his right arm in a sling, nodded as cheerfully as the surgical accessories permitted, and continued to limp along beside his mother, who was pushing a mercifully-sleeping Tyne in a borrowed pushchair.

"Not quite all," said Barry, who was surveying his empty wallet gloomily. "I hope the holiday insurance is going to cover this. I'll tell you one thing the hospital here is *not*, and that's cheap."

"You get what you pay for," said Shell, "If you hadn't been so tight while we were looking at that apartment this would never have happened."

"I don't know how you work that out," said Barry. "As far as I remember, it was you as wanted to go on about buying that apartment. I *told* you we can't afford it, and that should have been that. But oh no, you, Mrs keep-up-with-the-jet-set here, you have to give him the impression we're serious about it, and all of a sudden we're there nine hours, and he won't let us out!"

"Well we had taken up a lot of his time. He'd gone to a lot of trouble for us. Naturally he wanted us to get a good deal. I think he genuinely liked us."

"*Do* you?" said Barry meaningfully. "Do you *really?*" He didn't like us that much when our Roger fell off that scaffolding onto the half tiled patio, did he?"

"Well those girls shouldn't have gone home leaving the kids to their own devices should they? Disgraceful I call it. Anything could have happened!"

"What, like an eight year-old running riot on a deserted building site? That *did* happen Shell, in case it escaped your notice."

"You know what I mean. Something could have happened to the others too. Bex might have been kidnapped! You read about these things, pretty girls, on these holiday islands."

"They'd be welcome to her" said Barry, looking back at his gothic-clad eldest daughter who was scowling at her phone several metres behind them, having spent the last six hours sighing loudly every time it was explained to her that the hospital didn't have a McDonalds, a KFC or a Ben and Jerry's, and the wi-fi wasn't there specifically for her use.

"And there's Tyne," Shell pointed out.

"So there is," said Barry.

"Mind you I was surprised Degsy didn't wait until the ambulance arrived," Shell said.

"Yeah. One blast of an emergency siren and he was out of there like a rat up a drainpipe," said Barry, cheering up at the memory. "Must have something to hide."

"That apartment was lovely though," said Shell. "Perhaps we could go back and have another look later in the week."

"Ae you *mad?*" spluttered Barry. "Do you have any idea what a lucky escape we just had?"

"I never," said Roger happily. "I never had a lucky cape. I want a lucky cape! Mum? Can I have a lucky cape? Can I have ice cream? I want *ice cream!*"

"You've had a fall," Shell said. "And a lot of medicine. You won't be having ice cream for a very long while."

Roger began to wail, for the first time since his accident.

"He's not suffered any long term damage then," observed Barry.

"Poor little angel," said Shell. "Do you think we should apologise to Degsy? For wasting his time and then not buying an apartment? Perhaps we could pop in. On our way to the fiesta maybe?"

"Somehow I doubt he'll be there," said Barry. "At least not if he sees us coming."

Chapter Thirty-Two

Salty was woken by the sides of his bunk vibrating to a series of sharp knocks. At first he couldn't work out what it was, and wondered if he was back in his most recurrent dream, that he was running away from a band of pirates, who were mainly woodland animals, and one of whom, possibly the fox, but maybe the stoat, was shooting at him.

A gruff man's voice shouted a stream of largely unintelligible words, possibly including 'outrageous' and 'disrespectful of people's personal right to peace and quiet'. Salty recognised the dulcet tones of Francis, presumably woken from his own pirate dream on his own boat a few feet away.

There was a short pause and then the knocking began again, more insistently this time. Struggling into proper consciousness, Salty found his shorts where he had left them, by the bed, and put them on. Fighting a wave of weariness, due to rather too long spent at the Sailors Arms the previous evening, he stood up, and unusually for a man who spent his entire life sleeping in a space no bigger than an airing cupboard, hit his head on the skylight. Opening the offending glass panel, he put his head above deck. He could see along the length of the decking to the railing at the front of *Cangreco* and then out into the sea.

He turned 180 degrees and his eyes drew level with another pair of eyes, regarding him curiously. There was somebody standing on the pontoon by the boat, and that somebody was clearly trying to attract his attention. The eyes were a pretty blue, flecked with hazel, and decidedly twinkly.

"Hello?" Salty said politely, aware that he must look a bit silly, with his head sticking out of the deck like a meerkat peering out of a hole in the desert. Then again, it was a good thing the owner of the eyes couldn't see the rest of him, much of which was still technically in bed.

"Salty?" said a female voice. "Is that you?"

"I think so," said Salty, confused. "Who's calling?"

"Is Atticus there?"

"Atticus? I don't know. Probably. Isn't he in his cabin?"

"I don't know. I haven't looked. I was always told it was rude to board a boat without the skipper's permission."

"Good point," said Francis loudly from his own deck. "At least some people know how to ruddy well behave."

"You're right, it is considered bad form," said Salty. "Doesn't usually stop people though. Anyway, you're welcome to come up. If you want to. Hang on, I'll come out."

Salty's head disappeared inside the boat again, and within a couple of minutes he reappeared through the galley into the cockpit, pulling on a T-shirt as he went. He put out a hand and a pretty woman in a red and white striped top and a pair of navy linen trousers allowed herself to be hauled up. She felt a great deal lighter than she looked, he noticed, as she landed neatly beside him.

Mack, still soundly asleep in the cockpit with his head on the liferaft, snored loudly and long.

"Sorry about him," said Salty, "He's not the sort of houseguest we usually encourage."

"Hello Salty," the woman said, "You don't remember me, do you?"

There was something very vaguely familiar about her, but he couldn't quite place it, something about his youth, a summer moment, school uniforms in the park beside St Joseph's. She had asked for Atticus. But it couldn't be....*Could it?*

"*Hermione?*" he said.

Hilly laughed. "Got it in one," she said. "Although I'd have recognised you anywhere. You've hardly changed, except for the tan. I however, have doubled in size as well as in age, and I can assure you, there are numerous and distinct signs of wear and tear."

"Are there?" said Salty, "I can't see any from here. You look great. How long has it been since we last met, Herm?"

"They call me Hilly now. Everyone does. And for the record it's probably about twenty years. Although I shall deny it if anyone asks."

"I had no idea you were coming. Does Atticus know you're here?"

"I don't think so. It was a last minute decision really. There I was, sitting in a puddle in the UK, which is *vile* right now, all darkness and rain and grumpy kids, and I fancied a bit of sun. Atticus seemed to be having a good time, at least..." Here her voice trailed off, and Salty looked directly at her.

"Oh alright," she continued, "I never could lie to you. The thing is, he told me about your girlfriend, and to be honest, I did get a bit worried, especially when he sent me pictures of that party he went to. I mean he doesn't usually go to parties at all, and some of the people looked..well... sorry if they're friends of yours, a bit shady. I mean I'm sure they're not, but...And then Ma - you remember Ma - said she thought he might have got mixed up in some bad company, and he's been through a lot these past few years, so I thought I'd just...oh, I expect it sounds a bit silly now."

"Bad company? Party? What *exactly* did he say to you?"

"Oh nothing really. He said, in his texts, that he was having a good time."

"Good. I'm glad about that."

"Anyway, I'm here now, so I'll probably just say Hi, and then go off to the hotel I've booked and lie on one of their extremely inviting pool loungers for a bit, before I start to feel guilty about my husband and my children, and then I'll take myself off to the airport and go home."

"Atticus told me a bit about your family." said Salty, "Your husband and the twins. He's terribly fond of you all. Actually it sounds as though you've done everything right in your life Hilly. But then you always did."

Hilly looked at Salty's sad face. "Don't you worry," she said, patting him on the shoulder, which was awkward, as Salty was the best part of a foot taller than she was, "Whatever has happened to your girl, it will all work out fine in the end. Your friends are here to help. And speaking of which, is my lazy old brother still lounging in his cabin, when there's sun to be sat in and sisters to be hugged?"

"Come on," said Salty, leading the way. "I'll show you round the estate."

And then he saw Atticus's note, propped up on the galley table, anchored by an empty gin bottle.

"Ah," he said, opening it and scanning the contents, "I probably should have seen this sooner."

"Oh yeah," said Mack, who had come to, and was running one of his huge hands through his messy mane of hair, while the other was engaged in some rather dubious readjustment of the seat of his shorts. He looked like a bear which had just emerged from a long winter's hibernation.

"I saw Atticus going off at some unearthly hour this morning. Woke me up as it happens. *Bummer*."

"Right," said Salty, "this is a bit awkward."

"Did he say where he was going?" asked Hilly.

"Don't think so," said Mack, and headed for the very tiny cupboard known as 'the heads' which is the closest thing a boat has to a bathroom.

"Probably time to vacate the premises," said Salty, "Come on sweetheart. I'll buy you a breakfast and you can tell me what you've been up to for the last twenty years."

Chapter Thirty-Three

By lunchtime, Hilly had been given not only breakfast, but a thorough tour of the port, the harbour, and the many locals who populated it. She had enjoyed a hearty fry-up courtesy of the ever-reliable Jose at the Majestic, and caused some confusion amongst a few of Salty's friends who thought a) that she was Louise, returned at last, b) that Salty had moved on to the next girl rather too quickly, and c) that she was from the UK Inland Revenue. But there was no sign of Atticus.

Eventually, Salty took Hilly out onto the terrace of the Skyline, a rather swanky wine bar which was frequented almost entirely by tourists and was, as a result, rather soulless in the evening, but had a very pretty view during the day, when the same tourists were sleeping it off in their hotels or on the beach. He ordered two huge gin and tonics, and together they settled into some extremely comfortable steamer chairs and surveyed the scene.

"If he comes back to the boat, or into the port, we'll be able to see him from here," Salty advised. "But I'm sure he's fine. He's very capable."

Hilly looked at him.

"Do you think so?" she said, "I suppose as his sister I'm a bit over-protective. But he did have a terrible time after Flora. I expect he told you all about that."

"He didn't as it happened," said Salty. "But then I always think women overestimate the amount of time men spend talking to each other about relationships."

"So what *do* you talk about?"

"Oh, the usual stuff. Interesting things. Boats, Sports. Bars. Films and Books occasionally."

"We talk about interesting things too."

"Not the same things. Women talk about relationships and what things mean."

"What things mean?"

"You know. What he meant when he said *that*, or what he meant when he wrote *that*. Or what it means if he doesn't do the thing you wanted him to do. Or what *she* means by turning up wearing *that*, or what she really wants, although she says she doesn't want anything, and why doesn't he know that..."

"OK, Ok. I know when I'm beaten," said Hilly.

"But I can see you are a bit worried about the old man. To tell the truth, I feel a bit guilty. Dragging him all the way out here, and now it seems he's taken to the task in hand with rather more gusto than I had imagined, especially if he's as fragile as you say he is."

"No, No. You're right," said Hilly, "I am an old fusspot. And Atticus is a clever man, and if anyone can sort out where your Louise has got to, it's him. Leave it to him. After all, he was very brave in Venice. In the end."

"Venice?"

"He didn't tell you about that either?"

"Nope. I think he was going to, but then we got involved in a darts tournament at Lenny's."

"Right. Of course you did. Much more important."

Salty and Hilly sat in companionable silence for a while, as the bustling life of the harbour went on below them. The palm trees rustled in the light breeze, and a waiter brought them a fresh round of gin and tonics.

"Do you ever think about the old days?" said Hilly, wistfully, "You know, when we were all leaving school and the sun always shone, and everything was all about love and kissing and possibility?"

"If I do think about the old days," said Salty, after a minute, "I mainly think about you."

Chapter Thirty-Four

"Good heavens," said Hilly suddenly, a few minutes later. She sat up and inadvertently sucked in her tummy, which had become rather relaxed thanks to the gin and tonics. "Just look at *her*. Wow."

Salty followed her gaze. A small blonde was leaping out of a yellow open-topped sports car which she had parked recklessly close to the edge of the harbour. She was wearing a peacock blue silk shirt which fluttered round her and jeans so white that they almost blinded the many onlookers who had been stopped in their tracks by her arrival. The driver of a small grubby florist's van screeched to a halt and handed her a single rose through the window before tearing wildly off on the wrong side of the road.

"I'd give pretty much anything to look like that," said Hilly.

Salty stood up and leant over the railings. He waved.

"You *know* her?" said Hilly. "O.M.G. Is that *Louise*?"

"No, no of course not!" said Salty, "Louise doesn't look anything like that. Louise is beautiful."

"Blimey," said Hilly under her breath. "There's nothing like coming third before you've even entered the competition."

"That's just Pookie," said Salty, beckoning to the vision of loveliness.

"*Just?*" said Hilly.

"Darlings!" said Pookie a moment later, arriving on the terrace. "Thank God you're here." Her eyes settled on Hilly. "Salty? Whoever is this clever looking woman?"

Clever, thought Hilly. *Thanks.* She scowled, and then remembered her manners.

"I'm Hilly," she said. "My brother inherited the looks in our family, obviously."

"Hilly's brother is Atticus," said Salty.

Pookie's face lit up. "Atticus? Lovely lovely Atticus? Fantastic! I am so very glad to meet you. Atticus is such bloody marvellous fun!"

"Indeed he is," said Hilly, who privately thought of Atticus as more of the dreaming, thinking sort. "Bloody Marvellous Fun. All the Way."

"So where is he then?" said Pookie, accepting a large cocktail with a small tropical plantation in it from the adoring barman. "The lovely boy?"

"We don't know," admitted Salty. "He left a note, said he had something to follow up, and took the car."

Pookie frowned. "Oh dear," she said. "I probably should have told him. Been clearer."

"About what?" said Salty and Hilly together, "Been clearer about *what*?"

"About the Villa," Pookie said. "The villa where we went to the party. Billy Flynn's party."

"Wait a minute," said Salty. "I thought you said there was no party? Last night, when Atticus was talking about it, you said he'd had too much sun!"

"Yes, well I didn't want it broadcast all over the place that I'd been at Billy Flynn's. Some people might take it the wrong way. It never pays to be too open about things here."

Hilly sat up. "I find," she said firmly, "That it *always* pays to be *entirely* open about *everything.*"

"Ah well sweetie," said Pookie. "That's because you're a truly good person. And you're English."

"*You're* English," pointed out Salty, looking at Pookie.

"Not altogether. And not always," said Pookie.

Hilly resisted the urge to shout at her, fabulous silk shirt and pretty upturned nose or not.

"So, where exactly has Atticus gone?" she said, as calmly as she could manage.

"Well I don't actually know of course," said Pookie. "I mean I have no idea. Anyway he wouldn't have been so stupid as to go back."

Hilly and Salty looked at her intently.

"Would he?" Pookie said, her voice faltering, just a bit.

Chapter Thirty-Five

In books, Atticus thought, people come round after being hit on the head with a heavy implement and seemingly suffer no ill-effects, leaping up to solve crimes or rescue maidens without delay. As he opened his eyes, and saw the wooden beams of the roof above him, his first suspicion was that he was about to be sick. Fighting the urge, he closed his eyes again and tried to remember what had happened. He could smell a strange combination of things which didn't help; some sort of fuel, paraffin perhaps? Diesel? And paint, possibly. And something organic, like earth or grass. He became gradually aware of the ground underneath him, cold and extremely hard, like concrete. Something was digging into one hip, and he tentatively reached a hand underneath his body. Opening his eyes again, the room slowed down its spinspeed, and he saw he was holding a small garden trowel. A further inspection of his pockets revealed that his phone, the keys to Salty's car and his wallet, had gone.

The air in the building was hot, stiflingly so, making the chemical smells all the more sickness-inducing, and his head hurt like hell. He tried to push his fringe out of his eyes, and caused himself excruciating agony as his hand came into contact with what was definitely some kind of head wound.

He heard a groan, and imagined it had come from him, before realising that either his voice had gone up a couple of octaves, or there was somebody else in there with him.

After a couple of attempts he managed to sit up. He was in some kind of outbuilding, the late afternoon sun was still slanting across the floor through the wooden slats of the building, and as he reached out to one side, he found that the sides were warm to the touch. Along one wall were shelves, bearing cans and bottles of industrial sizes, with poisonous chemical hazard labels printed on their sides, and along another, a series of heavy-duty agricultural implements hung on hooks. Clearly this was a sort of garden shed, albeit for a fairly serious gardener.

He began to stand up but decided against it when the floor started coming up to meet him. He settled for looking round from his sitting position and that was when he saw a woman, lying on the floor at the other end of the shed. Her long chestnut hair spread out round her head, was matted on one side with what looked like paint but which just might have been blood. Her face was turned away from him, but he could see that one arm was lying awkwardly underneath her. Her feet were bare, and her jeans were torn at the knees. He suppressed the observation that they were extremely pretty feet, and began to shuffle over towards her.

There was something familiar about the hair, and as he got closer he felt sure he had seen her shirt before too, a pale pink cotton affair with heart-shaped buttons. The woman groaned again, and started to move about. At least she wasn't dead. Atticus had already had enough of dead bodies for a lifetime never mind an afternoon.

"Try not to move too quickly," he said, his voice thick with the heat and his own pain. "I think you may have a broken arm."

"Bloody hell," said the woman. "That's all I need."

"Here, let me help you," said Atticus, reaching her side. He put his own arm out and she used it to manoeuvre herself into a sitting position. "Where am I? Where are my shoes?" she asked.

"I'm afraid I'm the wrong person to ask," said Atticus. "I think we're rather in the same boat as it were."

"Oh. Boats!" the woman said with a small sigh. "That's where I should be, right now!"

"Me too," said Atticus. My friend will be worried." As he said it, he hoped it was true. The vision of Salty hosing down the deck of *Cangreco*, U2 blaring, and a gin and tonic waiting for him in a bar flashed before him.

"What day is it?" the woman asked. Atticus had to think. "I think it's still Friday," he said.

"Oh No!" wailed the woman. "That means I've been here nearly a week!"

"In this shed?"

"No. I was in a house first. A big room. Nice actually, lovely view and my own bathroom. But I couldn't get out. They brought me food every now and then. I tried to get out of a window but the room was up at the top of the house, and there was no way I could get down. There aren't even any decent trees this far up on this bloody island. I waited until one of them came to bring me food and I hit him with the in-room hairdryer. I don't think I even knocked him out, but he went down for a minute and I got out. He came after me, and I fell down the stairs, and that was the last thing I remember."

"Where are we?" Atticus asked. "Do you know who brought you here, who lives here?"

"This is *Casa Moreno*. Lovely spacious reception rooms, seven bedrooms, all en suite. Sweeping vistas to the sea, triple deck pool and poolhouse, over twenty acres. Well kept gardens."

"You sound like an estate agent," said Atticus as the light dawned. "I know who you are! Louise? Louise Renton?"

"That's me," she said, turning in surprise to look properly at him, and wincing as the pain shot up her arm. "You're right about this arm I think. Are you a doctor? I don't know you, do I?"

"No. But I know you," said Atticus, remembering where he had seen the hair and the shirt before. She was the girl in Salty's pictures, the smiling girl with the shiny ponytail who had captured the lone seafarer's heart. "I'm a mate of Salty's. From way back. School actually. He asked me to help him find you."

"He did?" Louise looked as though she was about the cry, "Oh Jeremy, the darling boy!"

"Jeremy?" Atticus was confused.

"Yes! Jeremy! You said you were an old friend?"

A vague childhood memory stirred itself in Atticus's brain. Salty's real name. *Jeremy*. "Sorry! It's been so long, I'd forgotten."

"He asked you to find me? Oh he is so sweet! And you've come to rescue me. You are clever."

"Not really," said Atticus. "If you notice, I haven't so much rescued you as joined you."

Louise began to cry. She leaned against Atticus's shoulder, and he could feel hot tears soaking into his shirt.

"They'll kill us both," she sobbed, "And then Jem will be all alone!"

"Now then," Atticus said awkwardly. "Try not to worry. I'm sure we'll work something out." But as the sun faded and the shed began to cool down, he had to admit he wasn't at all sure.

Chapter Thirty-Six

Hilly looked out across the harbour and wondered how she was going to manage to stay awake for the whole evening. In an ice bucket in front of her, two empty champagne bottles floated in now-lukewarm water. Pookie and Salty were deep in conversation about some point of yacht racing etiquette. Watching them, Hilly noticed how the blue of Pookie's shirt, the flash of the diamonds in her expensive jewellery, and the golden flecks in Salty's hair, all glinted in the sun, and merged into one, slightly hallucinatory whole. It was all very pretty and very warm and very peaceful. The heat had made its way right into her English-weather-weary bones, and her shoulders were beginning to descend slowly from round her ears to their rightful place, as if she was gradually, completely, breathing out for the first time in years. She tried to concentrate on why she was here, on Atticus and the possibility that he might be in trouble, but somehow, on this sun-bleached terrace, with the best part of a bottle of *Veuve Cliquot* inside her, the white yachts bobbing in the harbour and the low murmur of holidaymakers floating on the breeze, she thought, as Atticus had done just a few hours earlier, that nothing really terrible could possibly happen here.

She woke up when Salty put a large weatherbeaten hand on her shoulder, very gently.

"Come on Sweetie," he said.

Hilly struggled back into consciousness. "Sorry! I wasn't asleep. I was just thinking!"

"Of course you were," said Salty, "Thinking for two hours. Did you come up with any significant wisdom for us?"

"Atticus!" said Hilly as her mind focussed. "Is he here? Is he back?"

"Sadly no," said Pookie." And the thing is, I *do* feel responsible."

"No, No," said Salty, without much conviction.

"Yes," said Hilly, "It sounds as if you are. He's a stranger here, and you left him to go off on his own."

"Bird is his own man," Salty pointed out, "Pookie didn't tell him to take the car and go careering off up a mountain!"

"You told him you thought your Louise might be in trouble," said Hilly accusingly, "and you..." here she pointed at Pookie, "..took him to a party in a place he didn't know with some seriously dodgy looking people, and..."

"Hang on," said Salty, but Pookie held up a pretty hand. "No, no. I'm afraid Hilly is right. They are a bit of a dodgy bunch. We shouldn't have gone in, but I thought maybe we could find out if anyone had seen Louise. Dodgy they may be, but there is still honour amongst thieves."

"It sounds as if you should know," said Hilly, sourly.

"Either way, I may have, *unwittingly,* got him into this, so I shall get him out."

"How?" said Hilly and Salty at once.

"I shall have to use my network," said Pookie, "The trouble is, at the moment I can't quite work out who is on which side..."

"I think it would be far better if we went back to the police station," said Salty. "They may have some more information. And if they haven't, we need to add Atticus to the missing persons list."

Hilly thought she might cry, but then she looked into Pookie's impeccably made-up face, and decided she couldn't afford a mascara run.

"Right," she said, struggling out of the steamer chair. "I'll just go and, er, freshen up."

"I'll get some more champagne!" said Pookie. The other two looked at her. "To keep us going," she added.

As Hilly returned from the tiny and frankly inadequate bathroom, in that it had neither a mirror, nor any useful products for making a hot, tired, middle-aged woman look, feel and smell as fresh as a daisy, there was a massive thundering and rattling, and she feared the terrace was about to disintegrate and fall into the harbour. Coming out into the sun, she saw two huge men in board shorts and flip-flops with Salty and Pookie.

"Bloody English rugby players," said Mack, sinking into the chair that Hilly had just vacated, "Beer. I need beer."

"Bit of a handful were they?" said Salty.

"We didn't want to take them at all if you remember," said Mick. "It never works. Boys on tour. No matter what you set up, they just want to derail it. They must have rolled those jeeps ten times. It'll take a week to get the dents out and replace the busted exhausts."

The bar owner came out onto the terrace with a tray full of beer, which the two members of the jeep safari crew fell on as though they had just spent a month in the desert. Little more was said until they had consumed two pints each and the third round was established. Hilly and Pookie leant on the rail overlooking the harbour while the highly charged pair let off as much steam as possible.

"I think if we're going to the police, we should probably go," said Hilly, aware that she was sounding like a maiden aunt worried about missing a train.

"The boys won't stay," said Pookie, "In fact they'll be off in exactly four minutes."

"How do you know?" said Hilly.

Pookie nodded down at the entrance to the bar, at street level below them. Imogen Brookes-Turnbull, dressed in an optimistically short cerise kimono accessorised with a multicoloured turban was on her way in. Perdita and Lola were following, their dark-rimmed eyes deep with the effects of too much clubbing and not enough sleep, peered out from under their sulky fringes.

"Time to move on boys!" Pookie said to Mick and Mack, who were taking delivery of round four. "Posh birds on the horizon."

Mick and Mack downed their pints in one, leapt out of their chairs, and vaulted over the rail onto the flat roof of an adjacent building.

There was barely room for three in Pookie's little car, and although Salty gallantly offered to let Hilly have the passenger seat, his legs proved too long to fold into the tiny space at the back, so in the end it was Hilly who found herself squashed behind Pookie as they hurtled along the motorway at speed, veered wildly up the slip road, and descended into the town as if they were being chased by demons. Holidaymakers who had just woken up and were venturing out for a pre-dinner drink scattered right and left, as Pookie drove the wrong way round the one-way system 'so much more direct darling' and pulled up outside the grimy police station.

The policeman was just packing up to leave as they entered the dreary office. He sighed and took his newspaper out of his briefcase again, looking pointedly up at the clock.

"What you want?" he said.

"We want to report a missing person," said Salty, at exactly the same time as Hilly said "My brother's gone!" and Pookie said "We seem to have a bit of a problem." The policeman looked at them.

"I not understand when all spik together" he said. "Is stupido."

"He says we're stupid," said Salty and Pookie.

"I *get* that." said Hilly.

"Leave it to me," suggested Pookie. Salty and Hilly nodded. Pookie leant very low over the desk toward the policeman, who looked up at her, blinked, and took the lid off his pen.

"*Ahora Cariño, necesitamos su ayuda,*" she said in her most seductive voice. "*Estoy seguro de que, ll sabemos exactamente lo que tenemos que hacer.*"

"I think," said Salty to Hilly, "she's telling him she's sure he can help us."

"Well I'm not at all sure he can help us," said Hilly crossly. "Looking at the expression on his face, I'm not even sure that's what she's saying."

The policeman looked as though what Pookie was saying was that she would like to go to bed with him. She continued chatting away in Spanish, all the time fluttering her eyelashes and flicking her hair, while he wrote furiously in a notebook, pausing only to look up into her eyes for another fix.

"I hate it when women use their femininity to get what they want," said Hilly. Salty squeezed her hand sympathetically.

An hour or so later, with much flirtatious waving and kiss-blowing, Pookie ushered Hilly and Salty out.

"Well if that doesn't do it, nothing will," she said. "He says he'll get a team out to look for Louise and

Atticus first thing in the morning. He says he has had his suspicions that something is going on at Billy Flynn's place for a couple of weeks. He says he's already worked it all out. I think that last bit is a lie, by the way, he's hardly Columbo. Anyway, he also says he's right in line for a promotion, which means he'll want to get this right."

It was nearly midnight by the time Pookie dropped Hilly and Salty at *Cangreco*. The harbour was quiet, but life in the bars and restaurants of the port was just taking off.

"Come on you," said Salty, giving Hilly a boost up the steps and onto the boat. "You'd better stay here. You can have Atticus's cabin. There's nothing more we can do tonight."

Hilly, determined to stay awake until a)Atticus came back or b) she had worked out a plan of action to rescue him, lay down on Atticus's bunk, picked up his barely-opened copy of *The Lonely Sea and the Sky*, and fell asleep immediately.

Chapter Thirty-Seven

The thing about being a prisoner, Atticus thought, was that nothing changed from one day to the next. If he was right about it being Friday before it got dark, it was Saturday now because it was light again, But whether it was early Saturday or mid-Saturday, or in fact if he had been wrong about Friday and it was now Sunday, he had no idea. The shed had cooled down a bit over the hours of darkness, but the sun was already seeping through the gaps between the walls and the roof of the little building, and it wouldn't be long before it started to get seriously hot again.

"You awake?" he said to the back of Louise.

"Obviously," she said. "My arm hurts more than I've ever known anything hurt before. And I'm going to die soon. I'm hardly likely to be taking a refreshing nap."

"Sorry," said Atticus, "You're not going to die soon by the way."

"They killed someone. I know they did," she said. "I remembered. Just as I might actually have been about to doze off I remembered. They said they'd had to 'waste' him and that he would be food for fish. I've seen enough films to know what that means."

"I can't imagine villains really talk like that," said Atticus, thinking of the hideous, dead Webberly. "It was probably a joke."

"It didn't sound like a joke," said Louise, "but then somewhere along the way, I might just have lost my sense of humour."

"We need to try and work out what's going on," said Atticus. "Come on. We must be able to figure it out. And if we can do that, we can work out how to get ourselves out of it!"

"I've got a broken arm. You've got a black eye, and concussion I should think. We're both locked in a boiling hot shed with nothing but a lawn mower and a shelf of explosive chemicals for company. There's a gang of vile men out there who are talking about wasting people, and when, and if, they remember we're here I can hardy think they're going to open the door and say 'Sorry about that, off you go, have a lovely day.'"

"You say you've been here a week? How did you get here in the first place?"

"I've been going over and over that. I put the date in my diary. Darius, he's my assistant, he called me when I was on the way to work, saying there was a client up at *Casa Morena*, who wanted to be shown round. I said I couldn't go straight up because I didn't have the key with me, and Darius said the man had dropped into the office and collected the key himself. I was so busy yelling at Darius for handing the key over, that I didn't think to ask about the client."

"Darius gave the client the key?"

"No. He said Marge, my assistant, had handed it over before he got into the office."

"And you believed him?"

"I did wonder, Darius isn't the most likeable of employees. In fact I was thinking of letting him go. But he can sell, and business isn't so brisk that I can afford to lose a good salesman, especially if he goes straight to the competition. But I couldn't believe he would be so stupid as to hand a key to a client."

"So what happened next?"

"I called the office again, to ask about the client, so I knew what to expect but Marge said Darius had gone out. She said she *hadn't* seen the man, and that *she* would never have handed a key over without checking."

"And you didn't get suspicious?"

"Well no, not really. I just thought one of them had done something silly and I would have to do some serious training later. I headed up here to get to the client before he let himself into the house and started wandering about unattended."

"Go on."

"When I got here, I left my car a little way down the road, because I couldn't remember about the security. We have a code but only for the side gate, not for the main drive. I let myself in and when I got to the front door, there was a man standing there, holding out the key."

"He hadn't gone in?"

"No. He said he was waiting for *me*. I thought that was rather decent of him actually. I liked him."

"What was he like?"

"Sweet really. Quite short, a bit like a gnome. In a nice way. Whiskery. He had strange eyes though. A mixture of green and yellow. Like a cat. I thought he might be foreign. As in not English *or* Spanish. He had a rather loud shirt, and baggy shorts. He was carrying a coat though, which was odd. Mind you badly dressed men are hardly unusual out here. It's the heat. They just don't know what to do with it."

Atticus was aware of his own dishevelled appearance and hoped allowances were being made. Louise was continuing.

"He said he wanted a big place, away from it all, it a good view, plenty of garden and pools and so on. Said he was planning to retire from business and enjoy life. That's not unusual either. Many of my clients are looking to retire here. It's cheaper than mainland hotspots and the weather's more reliable than most. Plus there's the added advantage of a few places to keep large amounts of money under the radar."

"Did you show him round the house?"

"That *was* a bit strange, now you come to mention it. He said he knew what the ground floor was like, that he'd been here before, to a meeting or something. That he'd always wanted the villa ever since, but he hadn't seen upstairs. I was a bit suspicious. I'm always pretty careful with men and showing bedrooms, some of them have *very* strange ideas about what a female estate agent will do to sell a house, but he said he just wanted to look at the view from the master bedroom. We'd been chatting about his wife, and his children and so on. He said he was in cars, a 'big name' motor dealer. Anyway, I let him go in first, to keep myself between him and the door, left the door open and so on."

"So what happened?"

"He went into the *en suite* bathroom. Kept saying how spacious it was, and that he was just going to see how strong the power shower was. I don't remember anything else. When I came round, I was lying on the floor, all the doors and windows were locked, and he had gone. The power shower was still running though. Such a waste of water. I got up and turned it off, so I know he had gone. The rest you know. I hope nothing dreadful happened to him, he was quite nice."

Atticus was silent.

"The thing is, why do they want *me?* I don't know anything. I'm not part of anything. I'm just a property agent. I don't even know who's selling this place. We got the instructions and the key from another agent, who said he was leaving the island, and he had given the vendor the assurance that I would do a good job. Our instructions are to show the place, as and when we need to, get a sale and deposit the funds into an offshore account. When we get the word that the funds have arrived, we can hand the keys over to the new owner."

"That sounds a bit suspicious to me."

"Not to me. Not really. This isn't England you know. Money is different here. We've done deals like that before."

The sun was well and truly pouring into the shed now, like streams of hot syrup, thick and solid, crossing the floor. Both Atticus and Louise were sweaty and tired and it couldn't be later than eleven o clock in the morning. He knew they would have to get out as soon as possible, or there was a distinct possibility that they would die of thirst, never mind anything else.

He thought about Webberly again. He hadn't been dead long when Atticus found him, maybe a few hours. So if his calculations were right, Webberly was alive for some days after Louise was locked into that master bedroom. So why did they kill him? And more to the point, why didn't they kill Louise?

"When you were looking round the house," he said slowly, "Did you see anything else that was odd? Suspicious? "Like wooden crates?" Full of *guns*, he added silently.

"There were packing crates," Louise said, "but then there would be wouldn't there? Whoever owns the house is preparing to move out."

"Talking about moving out," Atticus said decisively, "We have to do just that." He looked pointedly at the rusting lawnmower.

Chapter Thirty-Eight

"You're more resourceful than you look aren't you?," said Louise a few minutes later, "Where did you learn to do that?" She watched, impressed, as Atticus finally managed to get one of the blades off the front of the lawnmower by gripping the wing nut holding it between the blades of a pair of shears and twisting. He manoeuvred the blade into the window frame, using a sawing movement. He had no idea what would happen, but the gap, albeit gradually, did get a bit bigger. Using items of increasing size, he wedged things from the shelves into the gap, to hold the planking, and eventually with a splintering sound, the frame came loose and the whole window could be lifted out.

"I built a wendy house once," he said, remembering a summer in Devon, a summer when Godfather Horatio was still alive, and Hilly was about seven, and the sun shone and life was just about fun and sticklebacks in jars and bike rides. He didn't volunteer the next chapter, the summer a few years later, when Godfather Horatio had died and the rain never stopped and life wasn't about anything much and he had set fire to the wendy house, which was the one truly wicked thing he had ever done. Well, until Flora. "It was all a long time ago," he added.

They both looked at the small gap where the window had been, and the splintering planking. Louise winced at the thought of manoeuvring her damaged arm through it.

"Look I'll go," Atticus said, "I can go and get help. Or find a way to let you out. Trust me."

"Good for you," said Louise in a voice a good deal braver than she felt. "I'll be fine. If they wanted me dead they'd have *wasted* me, right?"

Atticus leant over and kissed her on the cheek. "Brave girl," he said, "Not in a patronising way. I mean. You are brave. Braver than me anyway...."

Louise almost laughed. "Go on, you silly," she said. "I won't feel patronised if you don't get yourself killed. Deal?"

"Deal," said Atticus, hauling himself unceremoniously through the gap and dropping heavily down on the other side. He was out. Louise wedged the window back into the space in case anyone came past. She slid to the floor exhausted with the effort, and wondered if it was all a dream and she had been there all alone, the whole time.

Chapter Thirty-Nine

Salty sat on the deck of *Cangreco*, watching the Saturday morning take hold, and wishing he still smoked. The familiar sound of hoses on decks, which normally enchanted him, was an irritation, like a swarm of wasps, buzzing in the middle distance, and he was equally wound up by the sight of bar owners and tour reps starting to hang up the bunting and signage which would illuminate the Fiesta that night. Everywhere there was a creeping atmosphere of anticipation, even excitement. It was all very well for them, he thought, but he was alone. Louise had gone.

Every now and then, and this was one of those moments, Salty had to admit to himself that there was a possibility that Louise had not been kidnapped, or injured in an accident, that she was not even now struggling to get back to him, or trying desperately to find a way to call, or get a message to him. He had to face the fact that, whatever he wanted to believe, whatever he thought the past few months had meant to them both, there was the possibility that she had just decided to leave him. Maybe something - someone better had come along. Maybe he had done something wrong, and she had realised he wasn't the man for her after all. Perhaps it was the boat. It wasn't every woman who could imagine a future with a man who had no house, a bare minimum of clothes, who preferred a night on the ocean with a tiny galley, a non-existent bathroom and the wild stormy temperament of the ocean crashing round him to a night in a boutique hotel in the Cotswolds with champagne and the smell of an English garden in the breeze.

To be honest, he had been as surprised as anyone when she had turned out to be so very different from the way she looked. When he first met her, at some tour group freebie, apart from noticing her lovely, friendly, intelligent eyes, and enviable shape, he had also been aware of her professional self, the light, linen suit, the air of success, the glossy finishing touches, shoes, nails, hair, and the way she seemed to inspire confidence and energy in everyone round her. These women, those of the regular hair appointment and the walk-in wardrobes, were never terribly impressed by his 'old man of the sea' thing.

But somehow he had ended up standing next to her at the bar, and she had asked him what he felt about the ocean, and two hours later they were doing that thing when they couldn't remember where they had begun, or who said what or why, but they knew they just wanted to carry on, just talking, and walking, and eventually doing quite a few other things too. And Louise turned out to be more aware of the sea and more desperate to share the freedom it offered than many a seasoned sailor. It turned out they had plenty more in common too, from a love of U2 and vintage prog rock, and Mahler, to an equal passion for Jack Daniels on the stroke of midnight in a dark bay, or the freshest of fish, cooked on a galley stove within an hour of being caught, and Ben and Jerry's *Cherry Garcia*.

After a while, they became a familiar sight round the port, the sailor who was reluctant to go to sea, and the estate agent who was less and less often to be found in her office, a fact which the decidedly slimy Darius made a big deal of, whenever Louise's name was mentioned. Suddenly Darius took every opportunity to declare that it was really he who ran the business, that the women were really there for decoration, to 'charm the price up' as he delightfully put it. Louise had laughed when Marge drew her attention to it, said it didn't matter, because she had a *life*, whereas Darius clearly did not. Marge had been a bit less charitable about Darius, but then Marge didn't have Salty. Marge had Wilson, a stringy old rescue cat and Marge wasn't even Wilson's only mother. Marge had a group of loud and proud girlfriends, with whom she could barely keep up, and a dream of being swept off her feet by English actor Colin Farrell, who, she was reliably informed by Darius, had never been to Tenerife and preferred older, *intelligent* women.

If Louise had suddenly changed her mind, about the planned trip to La Gomera, about life on a boat, about *him*, surely, she would have said so, Salty told himself, again and again, and again.

Hilly, emerging from Atticus's cabin, to which he obviously had not returned, was equally low. She rustled up a weak pot of instant coffee and presented it without enthusiasm to Salty. Together they sat in sad silence, as the bunting went up on the neighbouring boats.

"Hey Ho," said Francis, who was uncharacteristically cheerful, hoisting a string of pointed flags up his main mast. "You two had a wild night on the teak?"

"Teak is presumably what Francis thinks is ocean going slang for tiles," said Salty.

"Oh God," said Hilly. "Do you think he thinks...that *everyone* will think....Oh Hell!"

Salty looked gloomily into his coffee. "It can hardly matter."

"Thanks!" said Hilly.

"Sorry," said Salty. "I know. It is annoying. But people we care about won't misconstrue two old friends sleeping on the same boat. This coffee's filthy by the way. Come on, we'd better go to Jose's place for some breakfast. "I have a feeling this is going to be a very long day."

Chapter Forty

There was a bit of a commotion at the Majestic because just as Jose's latest gloomy waitress brought their eggs and beans out into the sun, Sooze arrived in the Cupcake corporate mini, throwing dust over everything, screeching to a halt outside and demanding coffee, a bacon sandwich and some help. Apparently Amy's rugby team, buoyed by their exciting jeep safari of the previous day, had continued the action, using 'borrowed' hire cars to stage an impromptu rally through the villages and hill farms just above the motorway, and stopping to refuel with beer and tapas at every opportunity until they were eventually apprehended by the *Guardia Civil* and carted off in a police van to spend the night in jail.

"I suppose I shall have to go and get them out!" she wailed. "As if I don't have enough to do. Amy says the police won't listen to her, her Spanish is appalling, and Jules is nowhere to be found, *as per*. My schedule is already packed, and I've no idea how I'm going to get everything done. Barry and Shell and their terrible children are nowhere to be found, and Imogen Brookes-Turnbull says she just has to get a massage and a manicure/pedicure or she won't be able to go to the fiesta this evening at all!"

Salty took Sooze by the shoulders and sat her in his chair. Brushing the dust off his plate of toast he offered it to her, before signalling to Jose to produce more coffee. Taking the ubiquitous clipboard from her, he read aloud.

"OK. The Whites, and nice Rob and invisible Liv are all supposed to be heading up to look at the volcano at twelve, with lunch on the way, and back by four. Jules is taking that tour, and until we know for sure that he's not turning up, we will simply assume that he will. There's a minibus to collect them from their hotel? Sooze nodded. Right, well that should be fine.

Salty carried on reading the list. "Now why don't we borrow this charming woman.." he nodded at the waitress who was cleaning her fingernails with a fork, "..and get her to pop round to Cheryl at the Hotel Terraza to book the treatments for Mrs B-T so that she can be back, all clean and polished in time to meet the minibus when it gets back from the volcano. Then she can hitch a ride back to her hotel, and everyone can get ready for the big coach pick up, and back here for the start of the procession.

"The 'Funeral' procession starts here and travels along the coast, in coaches, buses, people's cars, carts, anything anyone can find. It stops in most of the smaller bars, on the way, and ends up on the long beach behind Los Cristianos for the big party," he added, for Hilly's benefit.

Sooze lay back in her chair and closed her eyes. "You are marvellous," she said faintly. "Will you marry me?"

Salty almost laughed. "Sorry old thing," he said, "I'm spoken for." Several people looked at Hilly, who shook her head rather too emphatically.

"Well I shall definitely buy you a cocktail at the Fiesta," Sooze said, getting up, "I feel much better.

Now I shall have to head off to the Police station. I'll see you later."

"Ah." said Salty, "Well the thing is, I'm not going. To the Fiesta."

Now everybody looked at *him*. "Of course you're going," said Sooze and Hilly together. "*Everyone* goes to the Fiesta," Sooze added.

"Of course we're going," said Hilly firmly, fuelling the port-wide rumour mill by putting her arm round Salty. "We're looking forward to it."

As Sooze fired up the Cupcake mini and sped away, and people returned to their breakfasts, Hilly added to Salty, "We *have* to go. Otherwise, we'll never find out what's really going on."

Chapter Forty-One

Atticus, now sporting a badly bruised ankle as a result of the drop through the window, as well as his black eye and an increasingly blinding headache, made his way round the shed. Given that it was being used as a high security prison cell, it was surprisingly ordinary, like the sort you buy in large garden centres in the UK. It was about two hundred yards from the house, and looking across in the other direction, he could see the swimming pools in the distance. He shuddered, remembering Webberly and the poolhouse.

However, as he pulled himself together and tried to concentrate, he found that the shed, ordinary as it looked, was rather better secured than might have been expected. There was a heavy chain across the door, and a fierce rusting padlock. He tried a few of his most basic lock-picking tricks to no avail, until he heard a noise. Somebody was walking across the grass towards him.

"Don't go away," he hissed through the door, hoping Louise would hear.

"Don't worry, I won't," she hissed back, as Atticus dived into a rhodedendron.

From inside the bush, Atticus had a significantly impeded view of the two men who came to a halt less than three feet away. One of them was smoking a foul-smelling cigar, his bare legs, in baggy shorts were pale and bristly, his feet, in ugly open sandals, looked neglected and dirty. By contrast, the other man wore well-pressed pale blue linen trousers and a pair of lightish brogues that Atticus himself might well have chosen. He couldn't see either of them above the waist, and the cloud of blue smoke drifted through the leaves and made his eyes water. Neither set of legs matched the pair he had seen earlier.

"All in order?" he heard one of the men say.

"All set Guv-nor," said the other "The vehicles are loaded, they'll be down at the jetty by twenty-two hundred as agreed. The boat'll be there."

"The boat a good'un? That's some weight it'll be carrying."

"Boat's sound. I had Carter look it over. It's spot on. Ordinary. Nothing to attract attention. And the owner's a good sailor too, which is handy. Nick Numpty fell overboard in a storm last time he tried to lift some kit off down to the Azores."

"Yeah, right, I'd forgotten Numpty. Found floating off La Palma a week later wasn't 'e?"

"That's the one. Anyway, not this bloke, He's a bit of an expert by all accounts."

"You're sure he'll do it?"

"I'm sure." There was a low laugh which made Atticus shiver, even though he was much too hot.

"If he ever wants to see *her* again, he'll do *exactly* what we say."

"Sorted then."

"Sorted. Although we could have done without Carter tackling the Englishman like that."

"Agreed. Should have done for that *'gentleman'* there and then. After he'd seen Spiders."

"Yeah. Shame about Spiders. I didn't mean to hit him quite so hard. But he was getting itchy about the girl. And when it's your time eh? He'd served his purpose, getting her up here. It's the way he'd like to be remembered, dying on the job, as it were. Lazy to let himself be followed though. 'E should have been looking out for the Englishman. I have to confess its a loose end mate. And I don't *like* loose ends."

"What are we going to do about them now, the gent and the girl?"

"Not my problem mate. They're safe enough for now in the lockup. Bit of luck they'll expire with the heat. Not used to it are they, these posh types. My job is to see the merchandise off the island. What happens after that's nothing to do with me. Anyway, Bill's got a team as does that kind of work."

"There you are then. *Sweet*."

"Yup. This is going to be one hell of a party. Funeral indeed. Ha ha. very funny. And *most* convenient."

The two men moved off in the direction of the poolhouse. Atticus held his breath. If the smoke didn't make him cough, he was sure to sneeze, with the pollen from the huge vulgar pink rhododendron flowers filling his nose and eyes.

Spiders. Spiders Web. *Webberly*.

Ordinary boat indeed. Salty would be most offended.

Atticus was still considering whether it was safe to leave the flowerbed, when he was even more surprised to see another, much prettier set of legs standing beside it Pretty legs, and even prettier feet, but no shoes.

"Atticus?"

"Louise!"

"Where *are* you?"

"I'm in here!"

"In where?"

"In here! Look out, there are *men* about!"

"I can see them. They can't see me. They're going into the poolhouse. You can come out now."

Atticus emerged gingerly, brushing leaves and dead petals from his hair and trying not to limp on his bruised ankle. Louise was standing in the shadows, her left arm now tucked fairly efficiently in the sleeve of her shirt, and looking, given the circumstances, rather marvellous.

"How did you get out?" said Atticus.

"Same way you did. I waited, and you didn't come back, and I heard those men go past, so I figured they'd got you and I'd better come out and rescue you."

"I was supposed to be rescuing *you*!"

"Well it's all a bit academic now. We have to get out of here!"

"Ah. Well yes. But...."

"But? *But???*"

"I think I'm beginning to understand what's going on." Atticus pulled Louise out of sight and started to explain.

Chapter Forty-Two

"So, if you're right, as long as we stay here, they'll let us stay alive so they can use me to put pressure on Jeremy - Salty - and they'll get away with smuggling their horrible guns off the island?" Louise said a few moments later, after Atticus had given her a slightly edited account of what he'd heard. "And then, when they get where they're going, they'll probably kill Salty."

"Well it's just a possibility," he agreed.

"But if we escape, and they catch up with us, they'll kill *us* straightaway."

"I should think so."

"And if we escape and they *don't* catch up with us, we're miles up in the dry hills, with no cover and no idea where we are, so we'll almost certainly get lost, or fall into a *barranco,* or something."

"Whereupon, if we're not killed by a thousand metre fall, we'll die of thirst or be eaten by wild dogs."

"There aren't any wild dogs in Tenerife."

"Of course there are! there must be! The Canary Islands are named after them."

"Yes well. If there ever were, they've all gone now. At least I've never seen one. Anyway, dogs or no dogs, it seems our only hope is to try and stop these villains, *before* they get the guns onto *Cangreco*, and before they stop *us*."

"That's about it. Look, don't worry. I'll think of something."

"*You* will?"

"Yes I will. Why does nobody ever believe *I* can be brave and clever?"

Louise put a hand on his shoulder. "I think you're both. In your way. Come on, we need to get closer to the house, and start by finding out how many of them there are."

"Absolutely," said Atticus. "That's just what I was going to suggest. What do you mean, *in my way*?"

"If only we could get a message to Salty!"

"Oh hell," said Atticus suddenly. "I've just remembered. My phone. It was full of pictures of the guns. There was an outside chance they'd think I was just some tourist, wrong place at the wrong time kind of thing. They'll never believe I accidentally stumbled into this, when they see those. They may even put two and two together and realise I know about the dead man too."

"What dead man?"

"Ah," said Atticus. "I didn't mention him did I?"

Up at the house, there were now four huge SUVs in the drive, their blacked-out windows and headlights glinting in the sun giving the impression of a pack of huge wild animals, crouching, waiting to pounce. As Atticus and Louise watched from what they seriously hoped was a safe distance, they saw three men emerge. Two were carrying another of the huge crates between them, the third opened the tailgate of one of the cars to enable loading. The crate was clearly heavier than the rest, and Atticus could guess what was in it. He could only hope there wasn't an empty one, left in the house, for him.

Louise pulled at his sleeve. Following her look, he realised that there was something happening in the road, at the other end of the drive. A vehicle, by the sound of it quite a heavy vehicle, was coming slowly up the hill.

"Help is at hand," Louise whispered. "Quick, come with me!"

"Wait!" said Atticus, "They could be more villains....!" But Louise was already inching down the drive towards the gate, creeping from tree to tree, to conceal her progress. He could do nothing but follow.

Chapter Forty-Three

"Now here, we have *Casa Moreno*," Jules was saying in a bored voice into the tour guide microphone, as the minibus approached the heavily padlocked gates. "This is one of the most impressive houses on the island. It's owned by a mysterious and reclusive film star, would anyone like to guess who?"

"Johnny Depp!" shouted Barry, "Bet it's Depp. He's reclusive alright, downright snooty if you ask me."

"He's *beautiful*" sighed Bex, without looking up from her phone. "Bit old. He don't live there though. He lives in France."

"Is it Ryan Gosling?" asked Lola, mildly interested. Perdita, sitting beside her in the minibus looked scornfully at her. "You wouldn't know Ryan Gosling if he came and sat on your lap," she said, "which he *so* wouldn't."

"Bitch," said Lola. "I only came on this friggin' trip to get away from Mum, and now I have to listen to you all day, whining."

"I think it might be Gerard Butler actually," said Perdita, flashing her bright eyes at Jules, who ignored her.

"They all live here, don't they?" said Shell, beside Barry. "Rock stars and film people and all that. This is the place to be. I said that just the other day, didn't I Barry? This is the place to be. We're buying a place here ourselves, as it happens, aren't we Barry? *Aren't we?*"

"Butler Butler, Butt means Bum!" shouted Roger from the back of the minibus.

"We are *not* buying a place here" said Barry. "*Not*."

"So go on then," said Rob quietly, from the front seat. Liv sank further onto his shoulder, flicking the inevitable strands of her long hair into his face. "Who is it then?" he asked, flicking the hair out of his mouth, "Who *does* live here?"

"Well, it's just a rumour," said Jules. "Although we locals like to think we're pretty good at knowing what's what, but the *rumour* is, it's Colin Farrell!"

""Wow!" said Shell, "We'll be neighbours! We'll have to ask him over, won't we Barry? We'll have to ask him for cocktails!"

"Who's Colin Farrell?" said Perdita and Lola together.

"Colin Farrell," said Rob calmly. "is an Irish film star. Brilliant. *In Bruges*, that's his best film. Although I liked *Seven Psychopaths* too. You should see them. Although you wouldn't understand them. Anyway Colin Farrell is in them. He is *not*, however, in that house."

Jules tapped the driver of the minibus on the shoulder. The bus slowed down almost to a stop. At the gate, the security man unhooked the small handgun he was carrying on his belt and aimed it directly at the driver's head.

"Mum, Mum, that man's got a gun!" shouted Roger. "He's doing a shooting Mum! *I* want a gun!"

"He has too," said Shell, looking slightly uncomfortable. "It won't be loaded, will it Barry? I said it won't be *loaded*. Just for effect. But then they need to defend themselves, don't they, these famous people. They don't want tourists gawping at them. That's what you pay for isn't it Barry? *Privacy.*"

The driver decided not to wait and see. He put his foot to the floor, and the minibus skittered sideways, before getting a grip on the hot road and re-establishing the slow climb past the house and on up the hill. In the undergrowth just a few feet back up the drive, Louise and Atticus could only watch, their hearts sinking.

Chapter Forty-Four

"You know," said Pookie, as they headed back to *Cangreco* after breakfast. "I'd have said it was a bit early to be dressed for the *Entierro*."

She pointed at a pair of swarthy men who were hanging around at the top of one of the pontoons. Both were dressed head -to-toe in black, in trousers, T-shirts and heavy boots.

"And that ageing rock-star-roadie look is *so* yesterday. Not the thing at all. And they must be so hot!"

Hilly looked directly at one of the men. He looked right back at her, and she felt sure she detected something more than a casual glance. She turned hastily away.

"I don't think they've got anything to do with the Fiesta," she said. "I don't think they're the party type."

"Nonsense," said Pookie. "Everyone's the party type. The key is finding one's own kind of party."

Salty laughed. "That's you all over Pooks," he said. "Although I might suggest that every party is your kind of party."

"Well I suppose black is still classic" sighed Pookie, looking rather pointedly at an enormous bald man in a straining pink T-shirt and some rather too-short shiny orange shorts.

"Well at least the cavalry's arrived," said Hilly suddenly. She pointed across the port to where a small police car had pulled up, disgorging four chunky uniformed officers. The policemen went into the Majestic, and could be seen moments later, at a well-appointed table, where they proceeded to order beer and Jose's famous rum-laced coffee.

"Good to see they're taking their work seriously," said Salty drily. Hilly noticed however, that the two men in black had disappeared. A quick scan of the scene yielded no sign of them.

"Do you think we should go and talk to the police? See how they're getting on?" she suggested, but Pookie and Salty were deep in conversation. She suddenly felt very lonely. She missed Hal and the twins so much. They would love it here, she decided. The boats and the beaches and the sea. Not so much the scary men and the police. Where *was* Atticus?

Suddenly, Salty who had sprinted ahead of Pookie and was already aboard *Cangreco*, reappeared on deck from the Galley. He looked wildly round the port.

"What? What is it?" Hilly said, catching up with him, "What's happened?"

Pookie had already vaulted over the guardrail with her usual athletic on-board efficiency. Noticing a piece of paper in Salty's hand, she took it from him, a moment before he reacted quickly enough to stop her.

Reading the paper, she went white. "This is terrible," she said. Hilly clambered, a lot less glamorously, up onto the boat and took the note from Pookie.

"**WE HAVE YOUR GIRL**" it read, in ugly black capitals. "**IF YOU WANT TO SEE HER AGAIN, DO AS WE SAY. BE READY TO SAIL AT 8 O CLOCK TONIGHT. NO POLICE OR SHE'S HISTORY**"

Underneath, as if writing a postscript in an entirely different handwriting, someone else had scrawled "**The bloke too. The toff.**" There was an ugly stain on the paper.

"Is that blood?" said Pookie faintly.

Salty looked more closely. "I think it's *salsa rocco*," he said. "Red sauce."

Hilly looked back the way they had come. There was nobody about, and across the harbour, she could see the four policemen, still enjoying their drinks in the sunshine.

"We'll have to tell them," Pookie said. "There's nothing for it. Come on!"

"*No!*" shouted Salty and Hilly together. "No. Wait. We *can't*. You saw what it said."

"Come on," said Pookie. "They don't mean it. It's just a stupid prank. You'll see. It's probably something to do with the Fiesta. The locals can sometimes have a pretty dark sense of humour."

"I don't think this is locals," said Salty. "At least not the kind of locals who dress up once a year and burn a model sardine to celebrate the fish harvest. It's the words. They sound decidedly English."

"Well who else could it be?" said Pookie, uncertainly.

"She's right,"said Hilly. "Not about the locals. I mean about the police. We'll have to find a way of getting help without alerting whoever has Atticus and Louise."

"What do you suggest? We can hardly run round to the Majestic and have a cosy chat on the terrace over a few beers, can we?" said Pookie.

"I have another idea," said Salty.

The girls looked at him.

"We could just do as they say. I mean, we don't know what they want. Perhaps they just want a ride. To get off the island."

"They could just make a booking with Cupcake Tours then," said Hilly. "This doesn't sound like a joyride to me. No. We can't let them get away with this."

Salty looked at each of them. "Right," he said. "Look, the note is for me. It's me they want."

"So?"

"So we sit here for a bit, as if nothing's happened. In case they're watching us.Then we split up. You two go in different directions, in case they follow you. They're hardly going to have a tail for all three of us. Don't do anything in particular, wander about, bit of window shopping round the port. Steer well clear of the Majestic. I'll try and find a way to get a message to the Guardia without attracting attention."

"You will?" Hilly said seriously, "Make sure they understand the danger Louise and Atticus may be in? And get some proper advice about what to do?"

"I will," said Salty.

As she followed Pookie at a safe distance, walking away from *Cangreco* and back towards the port, Hilly was sure she saw Salty writing something on the back of the paper, before he disappeared down into the galley.

Chapter Forty-Five

The minibus re-started after the third or fourth attempt, and filled the cabin with diesel fumes. The occupants, hot and dry after their walk round the arid volcanic landscape which made up the National Park, were fractious, and keen to get back to their hotel pools and ensuite showers. Perdita and Lola were making as much of a fuss as possible, throwing their hair about and stretching their long sun-tanned limbs in attempts to attract Jules, who was busy trying to count the White children, who seemed to number either two or five, as they clambered onto and under the seats, and tried to climb out of the bus windows. Earlier, Roger had stuffed his little brother into the luggage hold, and only a desperate cat-like wailing had alerted the driver to the fact, moments before the picnic baskets and passenger hand luggage was thrown in on top of him.

As they descended slowly towards the sea, Shell was anxious to point out the holiday apartment they had viewed, standing in the aisle and pointing to every building site which came into view.

"Jules, look!" she shouted, "Isn't that it? That's it! We're having the sea view one, the one at the top on the far side. Aren't we Barry? I said, we're going to be living there come the winter. It's so lovely. The bathrooms are completely up to the minute, aren't they Barry?....Oh No. That's not it. That's yellow stone. Ours is white isn't it Barry? White. Like a wedding cake. Oooh it's so chic!"

"Look Mum," shouted Roger. "I can see a load of men doing a robbing! Look!"

Barry got up to see what he son was yelling about, and the combined weight of him and Shell in the aisle caused the bus to rock. Jules hastened towards them, almost shoving them back into their seats.

"He's right though, the little 'un," Barry said, pointing to over the hedge at *Casa Moreno*. "It looks as though someone is doing that place over. We should do something about it, shouldn't we?" Jules looked over the hedge. Three SUV's with blacked out windows were moving slowly away from the house, as several men loaded crates into a fourth. Behind them the house looked closed up, the windows shuttered.

"I think Mr Farrell can probably manage," he said nervously, "But I'll have a word when we get down to the harbour. Get someone to go up and check."

"Mr Farrell," said Rob quietly. "I don't *think* so." He looked round and saw one of the SUV's pull out of the drive and start down the hill behind them.

"Oh Rob," sighed Liv, and spread her thin wispy hair out over his shoulder again. He hated the way she did that. "You're brilliant. You know everything don't you?"

The minibus trundled down into the port, dropping and collecting passengers and returning them to where they were supposed to be. Sitting in the little office at the back of the Sailors Arms, after a long and very welcome Skype chat with Hal and the twins, Hilly saw them go by, followed by two black cars, in a macabre sort of procession. It seemed the Canary islanders took this whole Funeral thing very literally.

She felt much calmer after speaking to Hal. The twins although unable to sit still for a minute and being completely confused about the fact that Mummy appeared to be on the television, and there were no prancing cartoon horses or exploding rabbits on the screen with her, had been very sweet, and neither of them looked injured in an serious way which was something of a novelty. But then Hal always seemed to manage so well when she wasn't there. He assured her he was missing her, but she got the impression the house was a bit tidier too. It was a shame he hadn't been able to contact Rebecca, so she could be reassured that her mother was alright, but then Rebecca *was* painting again, and she was notoriously bad about answering the phone, or the door, when she was busy. Hal promised to keep trying, and made Hilly promise to try and enjoy herself, and get some sun, and said he was sure that Atticus was alright, and neither of them mentioned last year's trip to Venice when Hal had said Atticus would be fine and he very nearly wasn't.

A third black 4 x 4 trundled past the window as Hilly shut the computer down. They were sinister vehicles, it was almost as though they were moving of their own accord, as there was no way you could see in, or see who was driving. She went out through the bar, refusing the offer of a pre-Fiesta cocktail from the barman who was already dressed up in readiness, and was sporting a 1920s flapper dress with much fringing, a feather in his hair, very pointy high-heeled shoes and a lot of badly applied coral lipstick.

The port was really coming alive as Hilly walked back down to the water's edge. A steady stream of traffic and pedestrians made their way into the bars and restaurants, admiring each other's costumes and ordering early rounds of cocktails, which mainly seemed to consist of neat spirits, decorated with fruit and feathers. Hilly had promised Pookie she would call in on *Grace Kelly* so that they could have what Pookie referred to as 'a starter', and Hilly could get into a borrowed costume, which Pookie declared would make her the most beautiful widow at the funeral. Which didn't sound terribly attractive somehow.

Salty had said he would meet them in Lenny's darts bar but had drawn the line at dressing up. Hilly hoped that by then all the horridness would be sorted out, and the note would already be with the police, as part of evidence to be used against whoever had been holding Atticus and Louise. She hadn't told the whole story to Hal on Skype, for fear of worrying him, giving him repeated assurances that she was having a lovely time.

"You worry too much sweetheart," he had said. "You should be enjoying the sun. I'm sorry about Salty's girlfriend, but sometimes things just don't work out. You don't still fancy him, do you?" he had added as an afterthought, and Hilly had had to spend the last five minutes of the call reassuring him that he, Hal, was and always would be the only man in her life.

Men, she thought as she got to the pontoon where *Grace Kelly* was moored. In the end, they're just like small children. They just want to be sure you're there every now and then, before going off with new and more exciting toys.

A long flatbed truck was engaged in a very tricky U-turn, by the entrance to the harbour, whilst a raggedy rock band struck up a series of disco hits on the back. 'Help' indeed, thought Hilly as they moved onto a Beatles' medley.

Pookie appeared on the deck of *Grace Kelly*. She was wearing a very fetching full-length black evening dress, with a small pillbox hat anchored on her head by a dramatic turquoise feather, and what Rebecca Flint Drake would have referred to as 'a little nonsense' of a veil fluttering an inch above her pretty nose. Ma would rather approve of all this drama, Hilly thought.

"Wow," she said, admiring Pookie. "I thought this was just dressing up. You look the real deal!"

Pookie seemed surprised. "Oh well," she said, "It's supposed to be a Funeral isn't it? I just put on what I always wear to funerals."

She handed Hilly a glass of champagne, which had a little black bow attached to its long stem. Somehow, although it was beautiful, it was a bit too much for Hilly. After all, no-one had *actually* died. Had they?

"I've laid out a few things for you in my cabin," Pookie said. "Pick whatever you like."

Hilly looked at Pookie, with her super-fit swimming/sailing/entertaining body. Here was a woman who sailed her own yacht, who partied with top people, who was of indeterminate-but-certainly-lower age than Hilly, and wore three-inch heels with the same grace as she went barefoot.

Hilly sucked in her tummy, ran a hand through her too-thin and rather dry hair and took a deep sip of the champagne. She was going to need it.

She made her way down into the heart of *Grace Kelly*. As her eyes accustomed to the dark of the foreward cabin, she heard the unmistakeable thump of someone else coming aboard.

"Hey Sweetie!" Pookie was saying to Salty, who had consented to a black T-shirt and a type of skirt made from a black towel secured to his shorts with safety pins. "You look very sexy. Like a sort of nautical Mrs Danvers."

"So what's the plan?" Salty said.

"You tell me," said Pookie, pouring more champagne. "As far as I know, everyone is meeting in the bars here, and as it gets dark, anyone with a boat takes as many passengers as they can find and sails round to Cristianos, where we can moor up and watch the fireworks from the sea. If you remember last year, the tour companies rented dinghies and rowing boats and brought us sardines and sausages from the beach barbecue. Mack and Mick are picking up a few crates of beer for my passengers, and I've got plenty of this.." she indicated the champagne. "What about you? Are you taking passengers?"

"Oh. Yes," Salty said, after a pause. "Of course. If there's anyone left. I've stocked up on booze too, and there are bound to be a few stragglers. But to be fair, *Grace Kelly* sounds a good deal more party-ish than I feel."

"You'll get into it," said Pookie reassuringly. "Everyone does. That's the thing about small islands, we're all at the same party really. Everyone joins in, in the end."

Below deck, Hilly tried on a few of Pookie's lovely clothes, before settling for a long black slinky tunic which should probably drape but sort of 'caught' on her hips. The effect wasn't too awful. She added a long floating silk scarf in grey, and a mannish, black wide-brimmed hat with a silk ribbon round it. She looked at herself, a bit at a time, in Pookie's tiny mirror. The effect was sort of Gregory-Peck meets-Morticia-Adams. At least her grey Converse sneakers were no more out of place than the rest. She emerged from the galley to see Salty looking bleakly out to sea.

"We'll tie the boats next to each other," Pookie was saying. "Then if you find it all a bit much, you can send your passengers over to me."

"Yes, yes," said Salty. "Next to me. If possible. I mean it might not be The wind direction. Waves and so on. Anyway, we'll see."

Hilly caught Salty's look. If anything it was shifty.

Chapter Forty-Six

"You know this really is macabre" said Atticus, back at *Casa Moreno*, as three six-foot-four 'grieving women' with enormous boots on came out of the house. Their black hats bowed under the weight of tulle and chiffon veiling, and all wore skirts which either billowed or clung, with neither being remotely feminine. One of them was wearing long black gloves, another brandished what looked like a cigarette holder. At one point a skirt blew up, revealing a large expanse of white hairy thigh in a straining combination of stocking and suspender.

"Are they supposed to look like women I wonder ?" said Louise, "Or is that the point. That they aren't?"

"Well they're certainly not like any women I've ever met," said Atticus.

"Have you met many?"

"Well my share I suppose. Although I don't really know what a share is."

"I should think women would like you."

"Should you?" Atticus was surprised. "I can't imagine why you would think that. I've never noticed them if they do."

"Well maybe you should look more closely. Women are attracted to a variety of things, and not necessarily the things men imagine."

"I'd like to believe that..."

Atticus was cut off by a warning hand.

"Ssssh! They're coming this way!" Louise hissed.

It was true. The hulking great mourners were making their way across the lawn, hindered only by their skirts, heading towards the shed.

"Oh Lord," said Louise, "What will they do when they find out we're not there?"

Atticus thought quickly.

"They need us, as security to make sure Salty does as he's told."

"Yes."

"Their plans are very much under way. So if they don't have the security they thought they had...."

"Yes???"

"They will have to resort to other means to make sure he goes along with them."

"Like *what*?"

"I'm afraid I can only guess"

Louise stifled a sob. "Oh my poor Jeremy!"

Despite the obvious predicament they were in, Atticus was still struggling with the Jeremy thing.

"There's nothing we can do. We'll just have to wait and see. And pray for a miracle."

And a miracle was just what they got. Another gust of the Canaries' famous sporadic but powerful wind, on its direct route from the Sahara, caught one of the widows' skirts and sent him sprawling across the lawn, tripping the others up as they followed. Atticus and Louise were tempted to laugh out loud at the scene which was reminiscent of an old Ealing comedy full of maiden aunts, but instead Atticus caught Louise's arm. She stifled a scream of pain as he put pressure on the broken wrist, and they both stood very still, willing the aunt-heap to be too caught up in its own difficulty to hear.

"Sorry!" mouthed Atticus, "Come on!"

They scurried across the lawn, keeping as much out of sight as possible, round to the back of the shed. Pulling the window out, Atticus boosted Louise back in again, and handed the glass panel in to her before following. Replacing the window which was already buckled with the heat and repeated leverage, they sank onto the concrete floor, hardly able to believe they had been through so much, and yet had ended up where they began.

Moments later they heard the lock and chain rattling, and the door was thrown open. The biggest of the widows was standing in the doorway, hat askew, and a good deal of foliage attached to his dress. This would have been more amusing had he not been pointing a gun at them.

"Up," he said gruffly, "You're coming with us."

They were an odd group as they made their way awkwardly across the lawn and into the last of the huge cars which had been there earlier. Atticus looked warily at the inevitable wooden crate behind him as he found himself on the back seat, squashed between Louise and the smaller of the widows, who was reattaching the black silk roses on his hat.

"Lovely frock," Atticus said, as cheerfully as he could, "Makes me feel rather underdressed. How about you Louise?"

His voice, meant to cheer her up, lay unanswered in the thick evening air as the car made its slow and gravelly way down the drive.

Chapter Forty-Seven

The car moved slowly out of the gate and headed downhill. It was agony to think that they were so close to being back at the port, where they would be safe, where they could get help, where they would be reunited with Salty and Pookie and the rest of the gang. So close and yet so far. But the car showed no sign of stopping, and as they reached the roundabout where the road branched off down to the harbour, it continued on in a straight line, leaving the bright multi-coloured light-bulb frontage of the Sailors Arms, with its terrace and its wi-fi and its good plain beer and food, behind.

Every time the car went over a slight bump, Louise winced, her arm getting more and more painful over time, and Atticus was increasingly worried about long term damage. He'd seen enough cricket and rugger injures at school to know that broken bones were best seen to as soon as possible.

"Look here," he said, in as authoritarian a tone as he could muster, "My friend is badly injured. She needs to see a doctor. Perhaps we could stop at a medical centre on the way?"

One of the widows actually laughed. "You think I'm stupid?" he said. "No doctor. Anyway, your participation in this will all be over soon and you can see all the doctors you like. One way or another."

Through the darkened windows of the car they could see the headlights of passing cars, the occasional bright oasis of a petrol stop, and, far below on the coast road, the twinkling and sparkling of small collections of houses and bars, gathered round bays and harbours. Everything looked magical, like fairy lights on a huge christmas tree, but there was nothing magical about this experience. From time to time a fizzing sound came from what Atticus decided was some kind of two-way radio, but might well have been a spitting tom cat for all the information it yielded. The two non-driving widows occasionally attempted to make some sense of it, pressing buttons on the dashboard and shouting 'Hello hello?' and "Over and *Out*' into it, but in the end even they gave up and swore at it instead.

"So we're meeting the *Crab* at the *rendevous*, where the *merchandise* will be loaded?" one of the widows said after a while, "Is *Red Cow* on target as expected?"

"Better be. *Big Pig*'ll never let it go if not," said another. "Now we've got the *piglets,* they'd better not leave us out of the sty!"

"Yeah, *piglets* have a habit of becoming a right nuisance if *left unattended.*"

"So we won't be leaving them unattended will we?"

"We won't have to if the *Red Cow* does what *she* is supposed to will we? *Crab*'ll be sideways and well out to sea before anyone finds out they were here!"

"So *Big Pig*'s on board for the trip? Who's he taking along for the ride?"

"Well it won't be you, that's for sure."

"Oh? You *know that* do you?"

"Let's just say, I'm *in the know* shall we?"

"You? I don't bleedin' well *think so*. I've done my time with the Pig, so I have. He as much as *told me* I'd be in at the finish on this one. Anyway he has to know who he can trust."

"And who can he trust? *You*? Hardly. Look what happened with Carter. I mean *Little Chook*. Pig trusted *Little Chook* and look what happened there!"

"That's different. Carter's different. Chook's *family*, if you know what I mean. Although I always had my suspicions about that. Seems he's a *godson* or something."

"Godson. Right. We all know what *that* means."

"You mean...?"

"I know what *I* mean. I'm just not *saying*."

"Can't be. I mean they're nothing like each other! Pig's well, *Big*. And that Chook, he's just a long streak of p...."

"Bacon! Right! So you see where I'm coming from? Mind you I *said* it was a mistake, letting him have so much responsibility so soon, I *told* Pig. You don't want small change in your pocket on this kind of operation. You need *sterling*. Chook could've put us all in the duckpond."

"Not Pig. Pig'd never end up in the pond. Pig's *Teflon*."

They continued in the same vein for a while, occasionally laughing at their own jokes, and inevitably getting confused by their own hilarious metaphors, but in the end it all got rather wearing.

"Well this lovely agricultural chat is all very entertaining," said Atticus loudly,   "but this particular Rooster might point out that you farmers can't possibly expect to get away with this."

"You think so?" said the driver, "Well, my oh my, aren't you the wise one? I wonder if you'll be quite so smart when we get where we're going."

"Yeah," said the widow in the passenger seat, turning round and revealing a very unladylike set of yellow teeth, "And you know what I'm wondering *Ladies*? I'm wondering if roosters can *swim...*"

The others laughed. "I know rats can swim," one said, "But they don't like it much And after a while, when they've swum and swum and nobody's bothered to fish them out of the trough, they *drown*, and nobody cares."

"Oh shutup, all of you!" shouted Louise her voice shaking with fear and impatience, adding "You started this," to Atticus, "You're just making it worse!"

"Sorry," said Atticus. "Just trying to...well...keep things light."

"*Light?*" said Louise witheringly, as another small row of village houses passed by, just metres away, unreached and unreachable.

The sky was darkening but there was still plenty of the island's trademark pink evening light, hanging low on the horizon as the dark procession slowed along the autoroute, The traffic thickened with a combination of tourists in hire cars, confused by the lane system, and locals in a variety of unlikely vehicles weaving and hooting their way towards Los Cristianos and party central.

At one point the convoy stopped altogether and Atticus looked out, right into the eyes of a child, strapped into the back seat of the car next door. The child's parents were shouting at each other in the front seats as the mother tried to read a map and the father tried to avoid being taken out by a tatty tanker overtaking on the inside. Atticus grinned hopefully at the child, but all the child could see was his own reflection. It put its tongue out.

Down at the port, Pookie's party was in full swing. There was quite a crowd on the deck of *Grace Kelly*, as Mick and Mack loaded slabs of beer and cases of champagne, and hopeful guests queued at the pontoon's head, hoping to be invited aboard. Pookie, still resplendent in her funeral outfit and bearing her champagne glass aloft, moved efficiently around, taking in fenders, untying lines and checking the motor was running smoothly, in readiness for the off.

At the last minute, Imogen Brookes-Turnbull pushed her way through the queue on the harbour wall and made a break for *Grace Kelly*, her two daughters in tow. All three were wearing little black shift dresses which would not have been out of place in a Chanel catwalk collection.

"Pookie is a dear friend," shouted Imogen, teetering along the pontoon in her gold high-heeled sandals, "Come along girls, you know how *dear* Pookie will worry that we aren't coming!"

Perdita and Lola followed in her wake, both having had the sense to remove their shoes and delighting in the fact that even without them, both were taller than their mother.

"Perhaps she'll fall overboard," muttered Lola, as Imogen was hauled unceremoniously over the rail of *Grace Kelly* by a passing guest.

"Or we could push her," she added.

All three were safely on deck, and Imogen already reunited with the reluctant Mick, as Pookie revved the engines and indicated to the various bystanders that they should untie the lines holding the boat to the pontoon, so she could move calmly and neatly away.

Behind them revellers spilled out of bars and made their way onto coaches and into passing cars, as tour guides and locals tried fruitlessly to issue helpful instructions and point out potential dangers. The owners of smaller boats attempted to weed out the passengers who were already so drunk as to be a real threat to seaworthiness. Salty and Hilly took a circuitous route back to *Cangreco* to avoid being followed by would-be crew.

"So what did the police say?" Hilly asked as they walked.

"What?" Salty seemed preoccupied.

"The police. When you went to see them this afternoon. With that horrible note. I expect they took you more seriously this time."

"What? Oh. That. Yes. They did."

"So? What did they say? What did they tell you to do?"

"Do? Right, Yes. They said I should ignore, it, carry on as usual. Go to Los Cristianos with everyone else, stay in a crowd, and they'll deal with whoever sent the note. Although they don't believe it was anything other than a prank."

"A *Prank?* What kind of a prankster would kidnap two innocent people and threaten their lives?"

"We don't know they were kidnapped. We don't know they aren't just lost."

"*Lost*? I can't believe you're saying this. Only this morning you were still sure Louise was in some sort of trouble. And if Atticus has gone to look for her and he hasn't come back...well it seems to me there's a lot more to this than a *prank*."

"People here are different Hilly. It's easy to forget that these are remote islands as far as Europeans are concerned. The nearest land is Africa. The Canaries may officially be Spanish but even the mainland Spaniards are a long way from home here. Values, priorities, the rules, they're not the same as ours."

"That's no excuse. There are still laws. And I'm pretty sure kidnap and blackmail are well outside them."

"To be honest Hils, I don't really want to talk about it. I'm sure the police are taking it more seriously now. And if we just do as they say, we can leave them to get on with whatever it is they have to do."

Hilly stopped walking and looked at Salty incredulously. "Leave them *to it*?" she said.

Salty turned. "Look, I'll be no fun at this party," he said, "I'll just potter about out there for a bit and come back. Why don't you go and join one of the others. You can still catch Pookie if you run. Or you could get one of the dinghies to take you out to *Grace Kelly*. You'll have much more fun. You really should go."

He walked on, and suddenly Hilly realised what was happening. Salty was lying to her. She ran after him. "No No," she said quickly, "No. I'd much rather be with you. To tell the truth I don't feel much like a party either, and we can be grumpy together."

As they reached *Cangreco,* Hilly got up onto the warm teak deck, before Salty could object further. He began to check the mooring lines and fenders ready to leave. Hilly thought fast. If Salty *hadn't* been to the police it must mean he was planning to go along with whoever sent the note. And if she challenged him, he would just make her stay behind. He wouldn't want to put her in danger. But if she pretended to believe him, well he would have no excuse for asking her to leave.

Her thoughts were interrupted by a shout from the pontoon. Sooze, in a black catsuit and catwoman mask was jumping up and down, trying to catch their attention. "Can I come with you?" she begged, "My customers are all drunk already and I've had to put them on a coach round to Los Cristianos. Not that they'll know where they are, but there you go. And I need to get round there to make sure none of them has a horrible drink and burning-symbol-of-fertility-related accident. Besides I don't want to miss the fun. Please?"

Hilly helped her aboard before Salty had a chance to say no. If there was going to be trouble it would probably be better if there were more of them, although Hilly was by no means sure that Catwoman would be much use.

Salty untied the lines and started the engine. Hilly and Sooze found a bottle of very decent red wine in the galley and took it up on deck, sharing it out into tin mugs. It was a very different sort of party from the one Pookie was having on her champagne and dance-heavy yacht, but it was a party all the same. Or it would have been, if it wasn't for the deep sense of foreboding that Hilly felt. And the look of grim determination on Salty's face as he steered *Cangreco* out past the harbour wall and into the evening sky.

There was a slight thud from inside the boat.

"What the hell was that?" said Sooze who was not a seasoned sailor and had no idea how many things could fall out of cupboards, or slide off surfaces in even the lightest of winds.

Hilly and Salty looked at each other. Neither spoke, not wanting to voice their innermost fears that the people who sent the kidnap note might actually be on board.

Slowly, a head and shoulders emerged on the galley steps.

"God, *Sorry,*" said Rob, rubbing a hand through his hair and blinking. "I must have fallen asleep. Are we going somewhere?"

Chapter Forty-Eight

Up on the motorway, the heavy car came to a stop by the side of the road. Atticus and Louise both peered out of the windows, trying to identify a landmark, or a possible source of help, but the car had turned off the autoroute a little way back and they seemed to be on some sort of side road. Judging by the lack of artificial light, they were some way from civilisation, and looking up towards Mount *Teide* a forbidding lump of black rock against the deepening blue sky, on one side, they were also still some way from the sea, possibly quite high up. In the distance Louise saw aeroplane lights, so they knew they were nearer the airport than they had been. That was about it for clues. They sat in silence, any sense of optimism the stop had inspired, ebbing away.

In the front of the car the two heavies continued to knock the hand-held radio about, alternately shouting into it and pressing its buttons. "You want an iphone," said Atticus after a while, earning nothing but a sour look for his trouble.

""It's not Cristianos," said Louise in a whisper. "We should have turned off. They're going on."

"What does that mean?" Atticus hissed back, "Any ideas?"

"Well if they *are* looking for a boat, they could try one of the bays," Louise suggested. "Or I suppose...."

"Supposing's good!" said Atticus. "Suppose away!"

"Well there is San Miguel," Louise said. "It's deserted. Wrecked really. But you *could* get a boat in...at least a good sailor could."

"Salty could," said Atticus.

After a while the men took out a handful of coins and began an ill-tempered game of spoof. Sensing their preoccupation, Louise and Atticus communicated with low-key sign language and raised eyebrows. Eventually Louise leant forward between the two front seats and tapped one of the men on the shoulder. "I need to get out," she said. "I need to use the bathroom."

The men looked at each other. Then one of them pressed the button which released the childlock.

"You go with her," he said to his mate.

"No way," said the other.

"I'll go," said Atticus, helpfully, opening the door on his side.

"You stay where you are!" warned the man in front, getting out of the car to prevent Atticus leaving.

Louise made a break for it, noisily heading away from the car. Immediately both men followed, and having failed, as agreed with Louise, to close his own door properly, Atticus was able to get out on the blind side. Ducking down, he followed a line of scrubby bushes and was able to get a good hundred yards away before the two heavies caught up with Louise, who protested extremely loudly and convincingly that she was just looking for a bit of privacy, as they brought her back to the car. There was a good deal of swearing and slamming of doors as the men realised Atticus had escaped.

"Leave him," Atticus could just make out on the breeze as one shouted to the other, "He'll get lost out here. We'll be long gone by the time he's found. *If* he's found."

Atticus just hoped Louise would be alright. Leaving her was one of the toughest decisions he'd had to make. Keeping close to the edge and avoiding any available light, he stumbled along the road back the way they had come. he hoped he'd reach the autoroute and the last service station they had passed before things got any worse for Louise.

Chapter Forty-Nine

"The thing is, she won't leave me alone," Rob was saying, as Salty steered *Cangreco* quietly out to sea and turned into the wind to head along the coast. The island was almost more beautiful from the sea, as it rose up in the pale purple evening light, the sun still orange on the upper slopes of Mount Teide, the highest volcano in the island chain, with the rest of the island spread out below it in soft greens and golds, their colour deepening as the light faded. Swathes of sparse agricultural land divided up the small twinkling hamlets which looked a good deal more magical by night than they proved to be in daylight, as locals struggled to make a living from the dry, volcanic landscape.

The mixed crew of *Cangreco* sat on the deck, drinking *Marqueres de Caceres* from their tin mugs, each thinking their own thoughts. Ahead lay the busy bright lights of Los Cristianos, and more unusually, they could see lights on all the beaches, as they went by, where residents and tourists started their bonfires and racked up their stereos for the dancing. Behind the sand, in the streets, there would be processions and impromptu busking, as the paper sardines made their way to their fate.

"I thought the holiday might do us good," Rob continued. "She was always on about going away, a beach holiday, and I thought if she got what she wanted, maybe..." his voice trailed off.

"How long have you two been together, you and Liv?" said Sooze.

"Two years," said Rob gloomily. "I don't know how that happened really. One minute I was getting up the courage to ask her out, the next, we were going to four weddings a year together, and each one we go to makes her more, well, I don't know, *cross* somehow."

"Cross?" said Sooze, surprised.

"I'm not sure it is cross exactly. She just seems, well as if nothing I do makes her happy. I'm just not that interested in colours of bridesmaid dresses, or how to choose those little food things that aren't really food you should have at a wedding. But when I suggest we spend more time apart, doing some other things, she gets even worse, crying and booking those mini-break things, or getting really *really* drunk with her mates and then coming home and telling me how horrible they all think I am."

"You know what I think? I think Liv thinks she's ready to get married." said Hilly.

"Get *married*? Really? But half the time she can't stand the sight of me!" Rob was confused.

"It just looks that way," said Hilly, suddenly feeling terribly old. "She's trying everything. One minute she's trying to entice you into it, the next she's trying to let you know she can manage without you, in an effort to make you realise *you* can't manage without *her*. She may even try and make you jealous."

"Oh *that*," said Rob. "That was last year. Liam Hadfield. Tosser. *As if.*"

"Don't you want to marry Liv?" Sooze asked sharply. "I mean if you don't, you owe it to her to tell her. Not keep her hanging on. That's not fair. That's not fair at all. Being kept hanging on, That's really *horrible*." She spoke as though her teeth were wired together.

"I don't want to marry anyone!" said Rob. "If I did, who says it wouldn't be Liv? I don't know. She's lovely really. In her way. But I'm not ready to settle down. I see all my mates, all dressed up in stupid suits that don't fit, in churches when they don't even believe in God, with piles of silly flowers and scary women in shiny dresses with stuff on their heads and their girlfriend all done up like someone else, and it all costs thousands and I just think, *poor sucker*. That's not right is it?"

Hilly tried not to laugh. "It's fine," she said, "As long as you just think it. It's probably better if you don't say it out loud. But it sounds as though a wedding's not for you. Not at the moment anyway."

"I haven't done anything!" Rob protested.

Salty, shocked out of the daydream he always fell into as he looked out to sea, looked sharply at him. "What did you say?" he said. "What do you mean? Who says you've done something?"

Hilly spoke quickly. "Rob was just telling us he's not ready to settle down in life yet," she said soothingly, "He feels he has a bit more to do first. Isn't that right Rob?"

Salty looked away again.

"I think I agree with Sooze," Hilly continued, "Up to a point. I think you should tell Liv how you feel. Then she can make up her mind too. Whether she wants to wait for you, or whether marriage and settling down is so important to her that perhaps you're not the right man?"

"There's no right man," said Sooze firmly. "I should know. I've been hanging around Jules ever since he got here, and apart from one night at the beginning, I mean I really thought he was serious or I wouldn't have...I mean I don't..usually. Never on the first date. Anyway after that he's done pretty well everything he can to avoid me. We work together for goodness sake. I'm his boss. Well virtually. And it makes everything very difficult. And now he's gone even more weird on me, says one thing and does another. Men. I'm finished with them." She looked pointedly at Rob. "They're all the bloody same."

"You might be right," Rob said after a little while, as if Sooze hadn't spoken. "I'm here, hiding on your boat, while Liv is probably already on the table in some bar by now, doing the dance of the seven veils and expecting me to propose to her. Because she says, it's an *auspicious occasion*. Bloody hell, she probably even wants me to do it in public."

Ahead of them a tiny flotilla of boats veered inland, heading towards the harbour at Los Cristianos. Sooze got up.

"I'll help with the lines and fenders," she said, making her way along the outside of the deck.

Hilly sat still. She looked up at Salty. "I don't think we'll be needing them just yet," she said quietly.

Salty held *Cangreco's* course, straight ahead, into the wind, away from the harbour and out to sea.
"You knew," Salty said to Hilly, as they motored on in the dark.

"I guessed," said Hilly.

"But you didn't try and stop me."

"Would it have done any good?"

"Nope. I have to do it. I can't take the risk. These guys are for real. I won't let them hurt her. Or Atticus for that matter."

"At least we know they're together. That's something. He'll look after Louise. So what do we have to do?"

"There's another note. Just after you went off to distract the villains, there was a delivery. Wine. I like a certain red, and I have it brought round from a mate who runs an import business. He's a decent sort. I'd forgotten I'd ordered it, but I figured it would come in useful anyway. He loaded it straight into the wine box downstairs. I found the second note when I went to check it was all secured."

"The wine box? How did they know you'd look there? Oh. Right. Of course they knew you'd look there. Well what does it say?"

"We have to sail on to San Miguel. It's further round, out of sight of Los Cristianos. Years ago it used to be a very popular marina, because it's quite sheltered. There's never anyone there now though."

"Why not?"

"There was a huge storm about twenty years ago. Turns out it wasn't as safe as everyone thought. The harbour wall was destroyed and a lot of very expensive boats were lost. The sea just offshore is full of wreckage, which is why divers like it. The harbour is very deep and there are no buildings left to speak of, just a few ruins."

"Sounds gorgeous. *Not*." said Hilly grimly.

"But there is a long stone pier which survived the storm. I'm supposed to tie up there. Whatever they want with me, it will be pretty easy for them to get on board from there.

"Do you *know* what they want?

"No. They say the boat is to be fuelled up, and ready to sail some distance. Also I'll be taking passengers. But I'm supposed to be alone."

"We'll have to get the others off."

"Agreed. But without telling them? How?"

"Unless you think we could take them on? The villains?"

"Are you kidding? These are serious people. This is my only chance of seeing Louise again. Of making sure she's alright."

"What if they don't bring her?"

"I'm not even going to think about that."

"Right. Leave this to me." Hilly moved across the deck and sat next to Sooze.

"Where are we going?" asked Sooze. "I thought we were all supposed to be in Los Cristianos? I should be. My customers could be up to anything by now. I'll be held responsible."

"A small technical issue," said Hilly. "We thought it better to sort it out away from everyone else."

"Something up with the boat?" said Rob, "Is it the engine? I'm quite good with engines."

"Something like that." Hilly said, "We'll probably need to get off while Salty fixes it."

"Get off? Where?" said Sooze, looking out at the dark shore. "There isn't anywhere."

"There will be," said Hilly. "I believe there's a disused marina just along the way. I think Salty's going to try and get us into it."

"I'm not sure getting off is such a good idea," said Rob. "I'm pretty sure one should stay with a boat unless it has actually sunk."

"I think that's only in case of a real emergency," said Hilly. "If the boat is taking on water. At sea. We'll just be tying up a bit further along. It'll be much safer on land for all of us."

"*Safer*? What sort of technical issue *is* this?" Sooze sounded alarmed.

"Oh nothing much. I don't know exactly. We could just give Salty a bit of space to sort it out." Hilly chattered on, wondering if she would ever get to the end of the discussion.

By the time Salty headed into the dark bay, their eyes had become accustomed to the lack of light. A weak moon was already lighting up the sea, making it a ghostly green, and the distant sound of parties along the shore carried across the water. Hilly shivered, imagining what lay beneath them in the deep dark harbour. Sooze fell silent, wishing she had gone to a better party. The catwoman costume was completely wasted here. Nobody would see her. *Jules* wouldn't see her.

"Listen!" said Rob suddenly. They all sat very still. They could hear the sound of a small outboard motor, growing louder as it approached. Moments later a single light from a torch flashed across *Cangreco*'s bows and up towards the deck. Instinctively Hilly, Rob and Sooze ducked to avoid its beam, heading down the steps into the galley.

In the moments which followed, the deathly quiet was suddenly shattered by a great deal of banging and clattering as the two occupants of the dinghy hit their fists on the side of *Cangreco*.

"Hold her steady!" shouted a male voice which Hilly thought she recognised. "We're coming up. You would do well to do as we say."

Salty put the engine into neutral and a tall man in dark clothes scrambled aboard. From her position under the galley table, Hilly could see the feet and legs of the boarder. The legs were long and tanned. The deck shoes looked very expensive.

"Well well, this *is* a surprise!" said Sooze suddenly, emerging from the fore cabin and making her way up the steps. Hilly, unable to stop her, followed.

Standing on the deck, lit by the greasy moon, Salty pale and silent was still standing behind the wheel. Facing him, with a gun aimed right at Salty's chest, was Jules.

Chapter Fifty

What the hell are you doing?" Sooze said furiously. "You bloody idiot! That's a gun!"

"I expect he knows it's a gun," said Salty calmly. "The question is, what he plans to do with it."

"That's it for you with Cupcake Tours," Sooze went on, "What about the Whites? Barry and Shell and their revolting kids? They've paid for the full Fiesta Night Out. You're supposed to be chaperoning them round the Fiesta, doing the full procession, dinner at Paulo and Maria's. That kid of theirs'll be up to all sorts. They'll be wanting their money back I can tell you. I know their sort. First chance they get they find a reason to claim compensation. And this is certainly a reason."

"Shutup," said Jules. "Just shut bloody up. This hasn't got anything to do with you."

"I certainly *has* something to do with me," said Sooze. "You're on a disciplinary for a start. "This is a sackable offence. Gross misconduct."

"Like I care," said Jules. "Cupcake Tours. Not exactly a job for a man is it? I only took it because you were desperate, and I needed a cover story. Jeep Safari eh? Not exactly *Thompson* are you? You going to do as I say or what?" he added to Salty. "You were *supposed* to be alone."

"I know," said Salty. "These people are innocent bystanders. I suggest you let them get off."

"Get off?" Jules appeared to be thinking about it. "No chance. My orders are to see you onto the harbour wall, make sure *nobody* gets on or off. So the rest of you better go along with it."

"Or?" said Sooze.

"Or. Or I'll use this." Jules waved the gun.

"I don't think so," said Hilly, her voice seasoned by years of dealing with twin toddlers. "I don't think you'll do that."

"I will," said Jules, stubbornly.

"You're not really a villain," said Hilly. "I'm sure of it."

"Just a crap tour guide," added Sooze unhelpfully.

"Don't you talk to me like that!" Jules said offended. "And don't think I won't use this. I've used it already. I've killed, and I'll kill again."

"Why don't you tell us what's going on?" said Hilly gently. The boy seemed increasingly confused.

"It's my Dad," he said eventually. "He lives here. Here and a lot of other places. Mexico. The Costas. Paraguay. I didn't have anything to do with him when I was a kid. I'm a fashion model as it happens."

Sooze snorted dismissively. "Like you're good-looking enough," she hissed. Hilly shot her a look.

"I got plenty of work. Shoe and leg stuff mostly. But the money isn't much. Unless you're A-list. And trying to get to A-list means hanging out with some pretty expensive people. I went out with Kate Moss once."

"Sure you did," said Sooze, wondering if it was true. No wonder he didn't fancy *her*.

"Then my dad called me and told me to get out here and make some cash. It was all going fine, until some car dealer bloke got in the way."

"Got in your way?" prompted Hilly.

"I didn't mean to shoot him. I just, well I just did. Anyway I missed. I was sure I'd missed. But the others, they said I'd killed him. Anyway, it's done now, so that's it for me. Don't you go thinking I wouldn't do it again. I'd shoot you. Or your girlfriend. Or that other bloke."

"Other bloke?" said Hilly carefully.

"The posh one. Proper gent. Thinks he's a hero. I can tell him, he'd better not try any heroics with my dad and his lot. That won't go down at all well."

"Kate Moss," said Sooze again. "Well she can have him. I never really fancied him anyway. Wait 'till Amy hears about this. She always said he was shifty."

Chapter Fifty-One

The stand-off continued, with each member of *Cangreco's* makeshift crew wondering if they could get the better of Jules. Suddenly they noticed lights on land, moving down the hill towards the waterside, and Jules, who looked more and more as if he wished he hadn't come, stamped his foot and began waving the gun around again.

"Onto the..er..pier thing," he ordered.

Salty put the boat into gear, inching towards the stone harbour wall. The lights on land got closer, illuminating the dust stirred up by the heavy wheels of the line of black 4 x 4s. Hilly quietly hooked up a few fenders to prevent *Cangreco* actually scraping the wall, as the first of the cars drew up. Two heavy men leapt out and began throwing lines around. Catching a rope with a spare hand, Salty wrapped it around a cleat on the deck, securing *Cangreco*, which came to a delicate stop. He turned the engine off.

"Right." said Jules. "Everybody stay where they are."

Hilly had had enough. Standing on the outside rail, she threw herself off into the water.

"Woman overboard!" shouted Sooze.

"Stay where you are," said Jules.

"Don't be absurd man," said Salty. "She needs picking up. It's very deep."

"She can swim can't she?" said Jules. "And if she can't it was a bloody stupid thing to do wasn't it? I'm not so easily fooled."

Hilly surfaced for a minute, gasping and splashing. She hadn't expected the water to be quite so cold. A small bow wave of her own making backed over her and she disappeared beneath the surface again.

"Bloody hell," said Sooze, "I'll go then." She dived off the boat towards Hilly, both of them surfacing together. Arms round each other, they trod water in the darkness.

As they bobbed about, trying not to attract attention, they saw more cars draw up, and more men getting out, unloading crates from each car and stacking them on the jetty. A few had torches, others worked in the beams of the cars' massive headlights. Occasionally in silhouette they could make out the figures of Salty and Jules, still standing on the deck.

Sooze raised a hand and indicated a rusting ladder, right on the end of the jetty. Both girls started towards it, still trying to avoid splashing, and Hilly for one was thankful she had bothered to go at least sporadically to the pool at her local gym.

Just as she was beginning to think they would never reach the ladder, surely the sea was so much more difficult than the pool, and she would *so* much rather not be wearing a dress, it came within reach, and trying not to notice its slimyness, and the fact that most of it had virtually rusted away into lengths of lethal looking sharp spikes, she began to haul herself out after Sooze.

Next time, whatever the theme of the party, I am going as a superhero, Hilly decided, hoping Pookie knew a good dry-cleaner.

They sat in the dark at the end of the jetty, getting their breath back. The men had begin to load the boxes onto *Cangreco*, and the pile on the jetty got lower as did the amount of yacht above the water line.

"Those boxes must be pretty heavy," whispered Sooze."Whatever is *in* them?"

Chapter Fifty-Two

"So you'll be celebrating then?"

Marge tidied up the files on her desk and replaced her pens in her *My Little Pony* desk tidy. Outside the office the street was already populated with revellers, who were starting early in the little bars and restaurants along the small promenade where Paradise Properties was situated, prior to heading down into Los Cristianos. Marge was in no hurry. She had agreed to join Shanae and her wild mates later, but by the time Marge got there they would probably be high on cheap cocktails and keen to go somewhere very dark and very noisy to meet men who were usually just looking for one thing, and it wasn't a romantic relationship. Anyway, they never fancied Marge, and frankly the last time she saw a man she'd like to go out with...well she couldn't remember the last time. But she held fast to her deep-set optimism, and told herself that she would certainly never meet anyone if she stayed at home. Like so many others, she had had a dream of island life, of sunshine, parties, plenty of casual work, and lots of young people to meet. In the end it wasn't so very different from Manchester. Except for the sunshine. Maybe that was enough.

Behind her Darius was rocking back in the chair in Louise's office, his feet on the desk, pretending he owned the place. Marge hated the way he did that.

"Sure thing babe!" he called out to her, "You can't hold a great man down! And I've a hot blonde whose Daddy is a millionaire, just waiting for me to collect her!"

The phone rang. Marge leapt on it, hopeful as ever that it would be a would be-date who had seen her somewhere and moved heaven and earth to get her number. Would it be too forward to agree to meet this evening? After all, any self-respecting woman would already have a date for the Fiesta. On the other hand, *she* didn't.

A woman's voice put paid to her imaginings, and she put the call through to Darius in Louise's office. She didn't really intend to listen in.

What was really odd, was the quiet. Darius wasn't speaking. He wasn't spinning lines, or making witty remarks. In fact he wasn't saying anything. After a few minutes he got up, and extending the phone line to its full extent, shut the door of Louise's office in Marge's face.

Marge switched off her computer and picked up her jacket. After all, it wasn't any of her business who Darius was talking to. She stuck the usual post-it note onto the door reminding him that she had gone and he was to lock up, and she left. Perhaps she would drive down to her favourite beach bar, further along the coast and have a drink there instead of going to the Fiesta. Nobody who was anybody ever went to San Miguel. but it was a pretty and peaceful place, and Marge liked it. She was beginning to realise she wasn't much of a party person.

TORA BARRY

Chapter Fifty-Three

Atticus scuffled along the side of the road like an old vagrant, Salty's worn shoes scuffing up the dirt and the rough rocks threatening to trip him up at every step. Clearly nobody bothered to finish building anything here, and that included the edges of a road. He could see a petrol station in the distance, its winking lights not really seeming to get any nearer, and he was periodically blinded by the lights of cars as they headed up and down the motorway. From time to time a speeding vehicle swerved violently towards him, lighting him up like a rabbit in the headlights, and causing much hooting and waving from the occupants. Everyone it seemed was in party mood. If only they knew.

As he walked he began to put two and two together. Where had it all begun? With Louise, missing from her office. Salty, convinced that a man in pricy deck shoes was following him. Then the party. Pookie had steered them right into Billy Flynn's villa. But she couldn't possibly have known that Louise was there. Could she? She knew who they all were. But Pookie? *Surely not.*

Atticus had vaguely heard of Billy Flynn. Even in his own sheltered and largely peaceable existence to date, in Devon, Cambridge, and London, the name was synonymous with some of the more serious international crimes of the last few decades. But that was another world wasn't it. A world a long way away from two old school friends, sharing a sailing trip.

Clearly Billy Flynn was up to something which required the assistance of someone beyond

264

suspicion, Someone beyond suspicion, *and* who owned a boat. Someone with a boat and a girlfriend who could be held to ransom. A boat and a girlfriend and a hapless old mate, who could, it seemed these days, be relied upon to find himself caught up in the middle of it all. *Again*. The pressure was on for Atticus to do something useful.

Another swerve from a passing pick-up truck sent him sprawling into the rough undergrowth by the side of the road. Much raucous laughter rang out above the noise of the traffic. *Not* terribly useful, he said aloud.

As he untangled himself, he became aware that a new set of lights was shining directly onto him, and these lights weren't moving. He put up an arm to shield his eyes from the glare. A car had stopped by the side of the road.

Atticus wondered about running. His legs were tired and scratched and he had twisted his ankle quite badly. But then again, if *they* had found him, he'd probably have a great deal more than a sprained ankle to worry about before long.

A large man got out of the car, leaving the headlights full on, so all Atticus could see was a silhouette. At least there only seemed to be one of him, although there was no way of knowing whether there were more of them in the car. The man approached, and shone a torch right into Atticus's face, which seemed frankly unnecessary.

"Steady on," said Atticus in as brave a voice as he could muster. "This is a very busy road you know. If you try anything there'll be witnesses!"

As if on cue, a minibus rattled up, slowed, and sped away, but not before a very lively trio in black hats and President Reagan face masks had a chance to lean out, make a series of very rude gestures and throw a variety of empty beer cans into the verge.

The man turned back to the car. Leaning in through the driver's window, and keeping the torch trained on Atticus, he turned the headlights off. Atticus could just make out what looked like some kind of uniform.

"You," said a voice which sounded vaguely familiar. "You from police station. You look for your friend."

"Thank God!" said Atticus joyfully, "Thank God it's you! Yes, it's me! I found my friend! but I was *right*, she *is* in trouble. Big trouble! We need to get down to the harbour, straightaway. There's a crime being committed. Several in fact. Possibly murder. Quickly!"

Atticus was halfway past the policeman and heading for the police car when he realised that PC Reluctant wasn't following him. Instead he seemed to be writing in a notebook, the torch held in his teeth.

"It is urgent!" shouted Atticus. "*Urgencia*?"

"What is your business here?" shouted Reluctant. "You know it is *offence*. Walking on road. Also dangerous. You are *vagabundo* I think. "

Atticus looked at Reluctant. "You know that job you were hoping to get? The promotion? I can *absolutely guarantee* you will get it, if you just do as I say!" he said.

"You?" said Reluctant. "What do you know? You are *tourist*." But he did put the notebook away.

"Well at least tourist is a step up from vagrant," said Atticus under his breath, and then more loudly; "Actually I am...er.. I'm an Inspector, *the* Inspector, of um, of..*Maritime Anomalies!*"

"What is this, Inspector of An Om Lees?" said Reluctant, getting into the car nevertheless while indicating that Atticus should do the same. "I not understand this English. Is like Inspector of Police yes?"

"Yes. Is quite like that," said Atticus. "And I am telling you to call for *Back up*. You understand? Help. More police. *Mas policias*? We're going to need them. A lot of them. *Mas Mas Mas!*"

The policeman started the car. With one hand he unravelled the police radio which had become tangled up in rather a lot of fast food wrappers in the footwell and with the other he turned the steering wheel full round, and put his foot to the floor. The car screamed its way through 360 degrees across all four lanes of the motorway. Vehicles slid to a halt all round them, and PC Reluctant sprang into life.

Atticus looked in the rear view mirror. The traffic was continuing on its way. After all, this was what passed for everyday driving out here.

Chapter Fifty-Four

Louise, sitting in the back of the SUV in the dark, waited. One of the heavies was standing guard, having been a great deal less than amused by Atticus's escape. From time to time he conversed with his mate, and even allowing for their almost laughable code-speak, she didn't like what she heard. Apparently Atticus would be most likely to fall into a *barranco*, one of the deep rocky ditches which characterised much of the island's landscape, or he would be hit by a car on the road, and nobody would bother to call an ambulance. Alternatively, he would go into hiding and die of dehydration. Or, he would be picked up by the police and thrown into a cell for vagrancy until someone remembered to sentence him to time in jail. Or, if all else failed, they would just hunt him down themselves, using their comprehensive network of serious criminals. And then they would *waste* him.

In the distance, she could see the tiny lights on the mast of a yacht, probably tied to the wall in the little harbour. Could it be *Cangreco*? The lights were correctly lit, indicating a boat on a mooring, not at anchor. Not many sailors bothered with that sort of etiquette out here, but Salty did.

There was a commotion, as several more of the gang ran back towards the car, shouting. It seemed somebody had fallen overboard, but it was impossible to work out who. The door of the car was opened, and she was dragged out. Her arm was agony.

The gang members were speaking in a combination of bad Spanish, very bad B-list gangster filmspeak, and lazy English. A girl, no, *two girls*, in the sea? And someone called Chook, who also seemed to be called Carter. He was dead. Or he would *soon be* dead?

Behind her, she saw the lights of more cars on the horizon. This alarmed the gang still further, and they began to run in all directions. They appeared to have forgotten all about her in their efforts to escape, piling into their cars, and accelerating off across the rough ground, ignoring the road altogether. Then with a squeal of brakes and in a huge cloud of dust, a police car drew up to where Louise was standing, dazed and blinking in the night.

Atticus leapt out of the car. PC Reluctant was speaking very fast Spanish into the police radio, while looking frantically round and trying to work out what was happening.

Atticus ran towards Louise, but to his surprise she ran away. He tried to follow, but she was faster, her long athletic legs belying how tired and dazed she was, as she ran towards the quay. Atticus was only able to catch up with her as she made it to the bow of *Cangreco* because suddenly, she stopped in her tracks. He followed her gaze upwards to where Jules was standing on the deck, pointing a gun directly down at her. Behind Jules stood Salty, his hands raised to indicate that nobody should move.

Two more of the gang were standing on the quay, having just loaded the last of the crates on board. "He'll kill her!" one of them shouted. "Nobody move!"

Nobody moved.

Just as Atticus began to worry that nobody was ever going to move again, he saw Louise step very carefully forward. Still looking up at Jules, who moved the point of the gun to mirror her progress, she carried on walking until she was level with the boarding point on *Cangreco's* starboard side. She reached up and caught hold of the stanchion, hauling herself up onto the deck.

"Stop!" shouted Atticus and Salty together. But Louise didn't stop.

"Let her 'ave it!" shouted the heavies on the wall, rather as though they were watching a wrestling bout on a wet Saturday afternoon in some East End dive. But Jules didn't fire. Instead, he tucked the gun into the waistband of his shorts, and dived neatly off the port side.

There was a scramble as the two remaining gang members realised they were on their own. PC Reluctant was heading down the road towards the water and in the distance, the flashing lights of more police vehicles could be seen leaving the motorway on their way down.

"Leave him! " said one of the heavies, "He'll drown. Or we'll get 'im later!"

An elegant white yacht with a blue hull, festooned with coloured lights and pennants, and bobbing up and down with the activity of a dozen or so passengers, well into a very lively party, sailed into view on the horizon and turned inshore. Pookie, still in full funeral regalia, was struggling to steer her course, given the distractions, but she persevered. "There you are!" she said, to herself, and to the absent Salty, as she held *Grace Kelly* steady, "Help is at hand my friend!" Standing behind her, a senior member of the Spanish *Guardia Civil* spoke quickly into his radio, placing his free hand reassuringly on Pookie's shoulder.

Suddenly there was a huge shout, and several of her guests threw themselves into the sea. Looking forward, she could see that most of them had chosen to leave their clothes on the deck. Apparently, according to Amy, who had been trying desperately to keep control of her rugby crowd, they had seen someone dive into the sea off a yacht in the harbour up ahead and had thought it was a cue to begin the skinny dipping. Half a dozen of the boys went in, followed by Mack and Mick, Perdita, Lola and eventually Imogen.

Pookie killed her engine, realising she would have to stop for fear of running her own passengers over in the dark water. *Grace Kelly* continued to bob cheerfully, in time to the chilled-out dance music she had been blasting from the speakers, just metres away from where Salty had just been reunited with Louise. On the quayside, policemen ran to right and left trying to catch the gang members, as Atticus shouted instructions.

PC Reluctant however, had other ideas. Standing beside *Cangreco*, he shouted in several mixed languages, the news that Salty was being arrested for smuggling guns. Salty disentangled himself from Louise's good arm, and they both got down onto the harbour wall. Immediately two uniformed officers leapt aboard and began to search the boat.

"Oh Hell!" said Atticus. "I forgot to mention that the skipper was a good guy. This'll take a whole lot of explaining."

"Not necessarily," said a very familiar voice behind him, and he turned in amazement to see two very wet women, one dressed as a mermaid, and the other as batman.

"*Hilly*?" he said incredulously, hardly able to believe his eyes, "*You*? What the *hell* are you doing here? And what *are* you wearing?"

Hilly held out her arms. "Hello little brother" she said, "It's been a bit of an adventure. But I am *absurdly* glad to see you!"

Sooze gave them a moment before stating the obvious.

"Sorry you two," she said, "This is very touching and all that, but we aren't quite out of the woods yet, are we? The police are all over Salty's boat and it's full of smuggled guns."

"Ah," said Hilly. "Well I was coming to that."

As she spoke they looked back at *Cangreco*. PC Reluctant and two of his colleagues were lowering themselves back onto the quayside, looking slightly confused. Amy, who had slightly more Spanish than the other two, translated their conversation.

"They haven't found anything," she said. "*No hay arms de fuego*. They say there are no guns."

"But I *saw* them!" said Atticus, "I saw them start loading, and there are no crates left on the wall. They must be on the boat!"

Hilly took his hand. "Come with me," she said, leading him rather wetly round the stern of *Cangreco*, where a strong inflatable rib with a powerful outboard bobbed happily, two people clearly visible in its depths.

"That's the last of them," said a female voice. "And just in time by the looks of it."

Atticus struggled to make sense of what he had heard. The dinghy's other occupant reached out and hauled them both into the side, hand over hand along the rocks. He scrambled onto the wall and tied the dinghy firmly to a heavy boulder.

"You again," he said, looking at Atticus. "I should have known you'd be in the middle of this."

"*Francis?*" said Atticus, vaguely remembering the ginger beard and the red sailing trousers he now saw in the dim light, in front of him.

"You're your mother's boy that's for sure," Francis added, reaching out to his passenger, "I thought I recognised that nose."

Hauling herself up behind him, wearing a huge multicoloured striped fisherman-style jersey, jeans and yellow wellingtons, was renowned landscape artist and granny, Rebecca Flint Drake.

"*Ma?*" said Atticus, "Now I *am* seeing things! What on earth.....!"

"I didn't know either," said Hilly. "I only realised she was here when I saw them draw up to the port side of *Cangreco*, after Sooze and I went overboard. They've been unloading every crate, over the far side, and rowing them over to Francis's boat. You can't see it, but it's just beyond the point."

"Beyond the point." echoed Atticus "That's rather how I feel."

Chapter Fifty-Five

Francis cast off in the dinghy, started the outboard and sped away, back to his yacht, taking evasive action to avoid the bobbing bits of Pookie's skinny-dippers, who were daring each other to race to the beach.

"He's alerted the authorities at Los Cristianos," Ma said, as if this sort of thing happened all the time. "They'll take the hardware into custody and deal with it from there. The police should have rounded up Flynn's mob by now. Although from what I can gather, nobody has actually seen Flynn."

"Ma?" said Atticus after a while. "What *are* you doing here? How do you know Francis? And you're not *seriously* telling me you have connections to Billy Flynn?"

Rebecca put an arm round her son. He could smell the unique combination of oil paint, linseed and Chanel No 5 which made up his childhood.

"You know sweetheart, parents do have a life outside their children's," she said. "And I had quite a life before you two even arrived."

"You are extraordinary Ma," said Hilly. "Even *I* didn't know you were here. I've been so worried about you!"

"I can't think why," said Rebecca. "Somebody had to come and sort this out. You were both getting yourselves mixed up in some very unsavoury business. Look!" She pointed at Hilly and Sooze, still dripping. "You're dressed as a tart and you're wet through. Atticus looks as though he's been pulled through a hedge backwards. Hilly, I think you and your friend need to find some dry and rather more appropriate clothes as a matter of urgency."

Hilly laughed. "Come on Sooze," she said, "Let's see if the boys have any spare kit on board."

"Can I just ask," said Catwoman Sooze, emerging from the shadows, "If you don't mind me saying, I mean no offence and all that, but you, Mrs..er..Hilly's *Mum,* you aren't all that big. And Francis, well I've known him for quite a while, although I've never seen him more than a metre from his boat, but he's not exactly a young man....."

"Your point is..?" said Rebecca.

"How did you move all those crates off *Cangreco,* and over the side?"

"They had help," said a voice from above.

They all looked up to see Rob, standing on the deck of *Cangreco.*

"*That* young man was *marvellous,*" said Rebecca, in a tone which made Atticus feel rather as though he wasn't.

"Wow," said Hilly. "Well done *you.*"

"I knew him when he was in the Foreign Office. With your father." Rebecca said.

"Rob?" said Atticus, who was beginning to feel completely drained of all sense.

"No dear, *Francis*." Rebecca sighed. "*Try* and keep up darling."

Chapter Fifty-Six

A while later, Hilly and Sooze emerged from the depths of *Cangreco,* dry, and dressed in a selection of sailing sweaters and shorts collected from Salty's wardrobe. Hilly unearthed another bottle of Salty's beloved *Marques de Caceres,* and poured mugfuls for Rebecca, Rob and Atticus. Gradually they began to unwind, as they stared out into the darkness towards the beach, where lights and excited noises signalled the arrival on the beach of several of Pookie's party.

Moments later, Pookie steered *Grace Kelly* alongside *Cangreco*, with the help of Atticus and Rebecca who proved to be considerably more nimble on the leaping-about front than she looked. Pookie stepped across the boats, a bottle of champagne in each hand.

"Glorious party darlings!" she said. "*Such* excitement. My policeman has just gone off in my tender looking very pleased with himself. "

"*Your* policeman?"

"Well between you and me, he's my brother actually. We don't see much of each other, he's a good deal too straight-laced for my liking but he can come in useful."

"So, *that's* how you knew about Billy Flynn, and all those other villains at that party!" said Atticus, with relief.

"Well, one's bound to pick things up, every now and then. At family things. You know, Christmas, birthdays, christenings and so on," said Pookie. "And I've found that it pays to know who your friends are out here."

"You can say that again," said Atticus.

"Hector, that's my brother, told me that Salty has gone with Louise to get that arm sorted out. They'll miss the party of course, poor loves."

"I shouldn't think they'll mind much, after all they've been through," Hilly said. Pookie looked surprised that anyone would be fine about missing a party. She picked up the pair of binoculars which Salty kept in a pocket in the cockpit. Surveying the beach she watched for a bit.

"Good heavens!" she said suddenly. "There's quite a fight going on."

Chapter Fifty-Seven

Marge had been frankly a bit put out when she arrived at her beach cafe, a scruffy joint a few metres from the ruined harbour at San Miguel. It was always a risk going there, mainly because it was more often closed than it was open, and when it was operational it was usually staffed by some equally unkempt local type who had little enthusiasm for the job. But Marge liked it because it felt unloved, and neglected, and by being one of its scarce customers, she could feel she was somehow sharing in its lonely state. And it was in a perfect place, having a lovely view of the old harbour and the cliffs, stretching away along the shore, and along to Los Cristianos, where fishing boats, ferries and yachts reassured her that life was still going on, albeit largely without her.

Now she found the cafe swamped by party goers, and impromptu picnics. Beer taps had been set up on trestle tables and in the back of pick-up trucks, and a few people were trying to light a bonfire. She decided to leave, and clutching the keys to her tiny rented car she started back up along the long track towards the road. In a blinding flash of light and a roar of over-revved engines, she was thrown sideways by a line of black SUVs being very badly driven away from the little ruined harbour.

Sitting in the dust on the side of the road, she found herself mustering a steely determination to go back and have a drink. After all, if the party had come to her place, they could at least find her a beer.

She fought her way to the front of one of the lively queues and collected a bottle in each hand, then elbowing her way back to the water's edge, where she settled on a rock. A few party goers shouted cheerfully at her, and although she couldn't really work out what they were saying, they sounded friendly enough. It wasn't so bad.

And then she saw him. Sitting on another rock, rather like her own, but a little way apart, in the dark, and entirely alone, was someone who looked a lot like Darius.

"So," she said eventually, having negotiated a slightly precarious route along the rocks to where he sat, "No party then."

She handed him her second bottle and he took it without a word.

"Truth is, there never is," he said eventually. "Not for me. I never get invited. I don't actually have any friends. People don't like me. I don't know why."

"That phone call," Marge said, "The hot blonde?"

"Ah," said Darius. "Yes. Name of Davina. I met her on a viewing. Daughter of some rich bloke who was throwing his money about. I thought she liked me. She agreed to come with me to the Fiesta. Then she dumped me. Said she had a prior engagement. She didn't though."

"You don't know that," Marge said reassuringly. "I expect that rich father of hers wanted her to spend the time with the family. Or perhaps she has a best girlfriend in need, and she doesn't want to let her down."

"I *do* know. It's not the first time. Sometimes I think they just say yes to get rid of me, then go away and work out an excuse. Anyway it's probably for the best, What would I do to impress a millionaire's daughter?"

"You could try being yourself," said Marge.

"Great idea. *Not*. I'm a nobody. I can't do anything except sell properties to people who are so rich they'll buy anything. That or just desperate to hide cash."

"Some of them are for real," said Marge, hopefully. "At least I try and think they are. That they'll love living in their beautiful home-from-home on the island where the sun always shines, that kind of thing."

"You really believe the brochure don't you?" said Darius, looking up at her for the first time. "The brochure which says Life can be Good. You're a good person. I'm sorry. I've been vile to you."

"Yes, you have," agreed Marge. "But you can always stop."

"What are you doing here anyway? Aren't you going out with that flashy mate of yours, Shanae?"

Marge thought for a minute. "No," she said. "I don't think I'll be staying in touch with Shanae. I'm not really her type of person. Or she's not mine. Actually, I like this." She indicated the dark rustling water, the winking lights of boats out to sea, the strange and unusual bustle of the little harbour.

"I'll get us another drink then," said Darius, struggling to his feet. "If you don't mind, that is. My being here. Only I don't really have anywhere else to go."

"Oh no," said Marge, "Anyone's welcome here." And as she watched him make his way over to the nearest beer crates, she thought how surprising life could be sometimes. He wasn't bad looking either.

That was the point at which Jules Carter chose to emerge from the sea, staggering with the effort of what turned out to be quite a long swim. Weariness overtook him as he reached the beach and he was only able to manage a few steps before collapsing onto the sand.

None of this appeared unusual to the number of people who were already leaping in and out of the sea, with and without their clothes, until the prostate stranger, still fully dressed, remained flat out, still not moving after a few minutes. The crowd gathered closer, obstructing Darius's way to the bar.

As he stepped over the body, he looked down and saw something glinting on the sand. Picking it up, he saw it was a handgun, and as he lifted it, Jules came round. There was a struggle, during which time any number of partygoers got involved, excited by what they saw as the first brawl of the evening. Only the arrival of the police halted the battle, by which time Darius had emerged as a conquering hero, who had managed to disarm a criminal on the run and thereby save the day.

"Wow," said Marge, helping Darius to his feet. "That was really quite impressive."

"It wasn't me," said Darius, I just tripped over the guy."

"Well we don't need to bother anyone with that do we?" said Marge.

"You know if Colin Farrell was here" said Darius, staring down at her with something approaching appreciation, "He'd be lucky to have you."

Chapter Fifty-Eight

"Good-O!" said Pookie, still looking through her binoculars from the deck of *Cangreco*, "That's the last of them."

"He was utterly useless as a tour guide" said Sooze crossly. Terribly vain and a bit stupid actually. I would never have gone out with him again."

"I thought he was quite attractive" said Hilly, "A bit like David Beckham. Not as attractive of course."

"Beckham *is* dreamy," agreed Pookie, "Especially close up. You know, when you get to know him."

"Missing the point a bit perhaps?" said Atticus. "After all, he did play a significant part in a gun-running and kidnap plot. And he did threaten the lives of Salty and Louise. Jules, not David Beckham obviously."

"And me," Rob added, "He threatened me."

"Quite."

"Not exactly husband material," said Rebecca kindly, to Sooze, "But then so few men are."

"I still can't believe that Jules is the son of Billy Flynn!" said Pookie.

"Is he?" said Hilly.

"That's what Hector said."

"I thought *Godson*" said Atticus. "At least that's what I heard. You know. When I was *kidnapped* and held against my will in a series of *very* dangerous locations?"

"Billy Flynn has a number of *Godsons*," said Rebecca, using her hands to indicate quotation marks. "And all of them have mothers who have been very stupid and let themselves be *led on.*"

"But not you ma?" said Atticus, "Surely not you?"

"Don't be ridiculous," said Rebecca. "I have *never* been remotely attracted to Billy Flynn. Regardless of his millions and his villas all over the world and his penchant for offering diamonds."

"Really?" said Pookie, "I never figured him for the romantic type."

"You young people don't know everything," Rebecca said. "But I said no, of course. 'No Billy Flynn' I said, 'you can keep your four-carat diamond. You went bad a long time ago.' He was devastated obviously. Never recovered it seemed. Went to the bad."

The others looked at Rebecca with renewed respect.

"So it wouldn't be a problem for you if you ran into him again?" said Pookie.

"Not at all," said Rebecca, "Although I wouldn't want to break the poor man's heart all over again. It wouldn't seem fair."

"That's a relief," said Pookie after a few moments, "Because right now, he's tied up and locked in my cabin."

Chapter Fifty-Nine

There was a roar of a heavy duty outboard motor, and *Grace Kelly*'s tender steamed back into view, creating a huge bow wave as it lined up alongside her port side. Two police officers boarded, scrambling down into her galley. Pookie sat unmoved on the deck of *Cangreco* as they all watched the scene unfold.

"It's a bit like *CSI:Miami*, isn't it?" said Amy after a while.

"Everything alright Brother Dear?" called Pookie occasionally, only to receive a muted "*SSSh!*" from out of the darkness.

"He hates me talking to him when he's working," she said, delighted. "He's already rather cross that I invited Billy Flynn to accompany me on this little trip round the bay. I knew Flynn would need to get to *Cangreco* ready for the off. All I had to do was suggest that he'd be less conspicuous if he came with me. Anyway, he wanted to be sure the plan was all going smoothly before being seen. *Ho Ho*. He never guessed I'd invited Hector as well."

The two police officers emerged from the galley, Billy Flynn handcuffed and struggling between them. They manhandled him into the dinghy.

"Bye sweetie!" shouted Pookie, brandishing her champagne bottle. "Nice knowing you!"

"*You* Billy Flynn have turned out exactly as I suspected you would." said Rebecca loudly.

There was a scuffle, as Billy Flynn, riled beyond endurance, made one last attempt to escape. In the commotion, one of the officers fired his gun into the air. There was a roar from the beach, as the revellers mistook the shot for the first firework, and began their own lengthy and dazzling display. All along the coast, parties of all sizes followed suit.

"That's quite a sight," said Hilly, admiring the coloured lights in the sky, as the police dinghy sped away.

"I hope Hector brings my tender back" said Pookie. "Last time I had to go all the way to Puerto de la Cruz to collect it."

"*Last* time?" said Atticus faintly.

Chapter Sixty

Hilly sat in the queue, ready to board their return flight, re-reading a series of texts from Hal. Rather gratifyingly, things hadn't been going quite as smoothly as she had suspected and the family seemed really pleased to hear she was coming home. Ben had been in Casualty with an almost-broken arm, after falling out of a tree, and Bill was staging a protest by refusing to eat anything which wasn't yellow until her Mummy came home.

Beside Hilly, Rebecca was deep in her book, a lengthy Russian classic which took up more than half the space in her hand luggage, leaving barely room for her large bottles of Duty Free Gin.

At the head of the queue, Amy and Sooze, both kitted out in full Cupcake Tours uniform, and apparently none the worse for wear, prepared themselves to receive the next consignment of guests, expected off the Manchester flight currently inbound.

"You know I'm really glad Atticus decided to stay a bit longer," Hilly said, "He really deserves to have a bit of fun, after what he's been through, and it will be great for him to spend a bit of time with Salty, and get to know Louise."

"Maybe he'll take a leaf out of Salty's book and get himself a proper girlfriend," said Rebecca. "It's high time. None of us is getting any younger."

"Thanks for pointing that out," said Hilly, "He'll find the right girl. When he's ready."

"He *had* the right girl," said Rebecca. "He had Flora. And look what happened there."

"Pookie was nice. I think Atticus took quite a shine to her."

"Oh she won't do. Nice enough I daresay, but I'll tell you for nothing, she's not the settling down type."

Suddenly there was a commotion as a small and very dirty child ran, hooting, across the concourse, like a Tasmanian Devil in a bit of a bad mood. Before anyone could stop him, he had ducked under the X-ray scanner and was headed for the tarmac. Barry, sweating and positively puce in the face, attempted to follow, and was firmly prevented from doing so by a pair of security officers.

"Barry? *Barry*?" shouted Shell, who was trailing half a dozen items of hand luggage, one of which turned out to be the sleeping Tyne. "*Get 'im!* I said *Get him!* He'll get run over *again*!"

A thin grey man in a loud suit appeared on the other side, carrying a struggling Roger. Handing the child back over the barrier to one of the security guards, the man attempted to hide his face, but it was too late.

"Degsy!" shouted Shell delightedly, "Oh Degsy, It's so great to see you again! We're so thrilled, aren't we Barry? I said we're so thrilled to see you! I wanted to say thank you for all you did. We're still *very* interested in buying that apartment you know. *Aren't we* Barry? *Very* interested. And when we do, you'll be the first to be invited. Won't he Barry? Oh..."

Shell's voice faded as the man turned away.

"Even if we did come back here, that tosser wouldn't be here," Barry said. "He's been sacked, that's what I reckon. He's going back to the UK. Look, he's on our plane."

"O.M.G. *Really*?" said Shell, "Well that's pretty rich. He told us he was doing so well here! Still, at least we can have a chat to him on the flight. We can ask him what his tips are for buying out here, can't we Barry? *Barry*? make sure we're seated right next to him, won't you? I said, make sure! *Barry*?"

"Shutup Mum," said Bex, without looking up from her phone. "You're so, like, *pathetic*."

Further back in the queue, Perdita was hugging her mother, somewhat reluctantly, kissing the air round her head whilst checking the concourse for nice-looking men.

"I shall miss you both *so* much," sobbed Imogen.

"No you won't," said Perdita, "In half an hour you'll be off with that Marco, or Pedro or whatever his name is. And don't think we'll be coming back to see you. This place is nothing like as cool as Antigua."

"And we'll get to do some *real* sailing," Lola pointed out. "Whereas *you* are going end up running a surf banana business with a man half your age."

"*You'll* be my age one day," said Imogen acidly.

"Never," said Lola, adding "Oh, and I'm getting an upgrade on the flight, by the way. Dad says I can. Bye Mum!"

"Upgrade?" screeched Perdita, "*Upgrade? She's* getting an upgrade? Not without me she isn't. Wait, *wait!*" Both girls skittered across the concourse to the ticketing desk their long legs bracing with the shocks delivered by their ludicrously high-heeled sandals, all thoughts of Tenerife and their mother, forgotten.

The passengers began to board the afternoon flight back to Manchester, where according to the whey-faced, flight-and-life-weary incoming passengers, it was just 12 degrees and raining. Behind Shell and Barry, who were still shedding children and tasteless souvenirs at every turn, was a thin, tired-looking girl shuffling along at the end of the line. Every now and then she looked behind her, as if she was expecting to see something, or someone else. But nobody came.

As they finally got onto the plane, Liv tried to ignore the empty seat next to her, while the others stowed their hand luggage and battled for window seats, and demanded pillows and Coke and extra storage space from the harassed looking crew. As the doors closed, the crew strapped themselves into their little seats for take-off, and the plane began to taxi slowly towards the end of the runway, she lay down across the two seats and stared up at the ceiling. Above her a little light winked on and off. 'Summon help' it read. But she couldn't be bothered. In her handbag, the tiny solitaire diamond ring she had chosen from the jeweller in her home town and had carried all the way out to Tenerife in hope, sat in its unopened box.

EPILOGUE

Salty steered a steady course out of the harbour and into the breeze. Ahead in the distance, rising out of the last of the morning mist, was the beautiful island of La Gomera, with its promise of peaceful bays, green forest walks, small hamlets and fishing villages. Beloved of locals and the better-informed tourists, La Gomera, without an airport, remained unspoiled, and as Louise said, they could all do with a few days of total peace and quiet.

Atticus had protested that they couldn't possibly want him along on their romantic trip, but Salty had insisted. Atticus however had taken the time to book a room in the island's least-famous hotel, from where he planned to walk and think, and sunbathe, and maybe even to read. *The Lonely Sea and the Sky* was still tucked into the pocket of his holdall, untouched and ready, although he wasn't at all sure Sir Francis Chichester would have much to teach him now.

They sailed quietly along the coast for a bit, drawing level with the bay where they had all been swimming just a few days, and a whole lot of adventure, ago.

"Look!" said Louise, pointing, "*Grace Kelly!*"

They looked over to where the pretty blue yacht bobbed at anchor. On the deck they could just make out the figure of Pookie, in her red swimming costume, reclining on the deck, her customary champagne glass in hand. But she was not alone. Beside her, a panama hat perched at a rakish angle on his head, and in his instantly recognisable pink trousers, was Francis.

"Well who'd have thought it?" said Atticus.

"Did either of you ever find out," Louise asked them "What her real name is?"

"It's Pookie, isn't it?" said Salty in surprise.

"It can't be!" said Atticus, "Nobody is really called Pookie. *Are* they?"

Just as Salty gave the signal to go about, hauling sails and tightening lines on winches in readiness for the long straight haul out to Gomera, he looked up at the cliff face, pock-marked with its hundreds of centuries-old caves. Right on the edge of the rock, legs swinging, a long, long way above sea level, and wearing a very odd sort of kaftan, was a figure he thought he recognised.

And up there on that ledge, the figure looked down at Salty, and waved.

Wasn't that *Rob*?" said Atticus.

THE END

Also by Tora Barry:

Going Going Gondola : An Atticus Drake Mystery

Mid-Atlantic

Atticus Drake will be back soon in:
A Bite of the Big Apple
In the meantime, why not visit
www.torabarry.co.uk for news of upcoming
publications, promotions and the writer's blog.

ACKNOWLEDGMENTS

My thanks this time to the following people, whose help and support make Atticus's adventures possible:

To Chris Howard, for another inspired cover, and to Katharine Fenton for friendship, honesty and skilled editorship. To everyone who read reviewed and commented on Atticus's first outing, *Going Going Gondola*, and in particular to those of you who took the time to tell me you enjoyed it. To all the friends I found in the Canary Islands, many of whom are still there, and in particular to Sharon Stevens-Craven, whose friendship and generosity made a return visit to Tenerife both a possibility and a great joy. To my own Salty, with thanks for all the happy maritime adventures, and always and for ever, JKEH.